GROWING hope

GROWING hope

ISBN 13: 978-1503155862
ISBN-10: 1503155862
BISAC: Fiction / Fantasy / Contemporary

Thank You

To Ryan: You are the love of my life. Thank you for focusing so much energy on helping me promote my books. Without you, my life would be incomplete.

To Madee, Heather and Kyndal: You are three of the best friends I could ever ask for. You've encouraged and supported me, laughed and joked with me and shown me that family doesn't mean blood.

To my parents: Thank you for always encouraging my creativity and being there when I need to walk through my crazy ideas.

To the fans: It means so much to me to have you read my work. Thank you for reading, sharing and leaving reviews!

GROWING hope

Prologue

Dorian took a deep breath and rubbed his hands together. The Creator had given him a job. He had called for the Council of Immortals to come to the Great Hall in order to ask for their help. The creation of man had been successful and it seemed to be bringing the results the Creator had hoped. The first men he had placed in each area of the world had been flourishing in their environments. Now was the time to create women.

He waited patiently for the others of his kind to arrive so they could begin their task. He heard them coming up the stairs of the great hall, their footsteps echoing off the stone walls around him. They entered the great hall and took their places around the large marble table.

"Thank you for arriving so quickly." Dorian said, nodding at each of them in turn.

"You called for us. We took an oath to come when you called." Lucien told him.

"The Creator has asked us to give of ourselves. He has asked us to help him create life." Dorian told them.

A sharp intake of breath came from the few closest to him. This was the first time the Creator had asked them to help with one of his creations. Perhaps he felt they would be able to offer insight into the female version of mankind.

"What can we do?" Asked Lida as she leaned forward eagerly.

Dorian explained the plan. The Creator had asked that they imbue woman with a piece of each of them. When man came into existence, he was created for survival. Man was strong, brave, and resilient. But man needed a companion to bring balance to the world. The Creator had made the Council of Immortals before he decided to create man. The Council of Immortals had become his confidants. Dorian knew that they had only been the first of many great creations.

In the beginning, they only existed as beings within the mind of the Creator. As the universe began to take shape, the Creator decided to give physical substance to the Council of Immortals. He had been pleased and surprised to find them all so different. Their physical appearances varied greatly, and there were a few among their number who were of a softer form. These were first females of any race, the first time the Creator decided there needed to be two forms in order to multiply.

"She should be kind." Charis said softly.

"She should be curious." Lida said with excitement.

"She must be loving." Caprice shared, smiling at Silas.

And so the discussion continued as the Council of Immortals discussed the characteristics best suited for a woman of the human race. Dorian smiled at the others of his race as they sat in their high backed chairs. The air changed, he closed his eyes waiting for the smell to hit him. He had learned that the experience was different for each of them, but for him, it was always filled with the crisp salty scent of the ocean. Taking a deep breath through his nose, he smiled to himself as he heard his brothers and sisters doing the same. He opened his eyes and found himself staring at the Creator.

He was a non-descript man. He had the kind of face and build that would lead anyone to believe they had seen him somewhere before. They had given up trying to describe how he appeared to each other because each of them saw him differently. The Creator smiled at them in greeting.

"Are you ready to see the woman come into being?" He asked serenely.

"We are." They said together.

The Creator waved his right hand and a man appeared before them. It was Epimetheus. Dorian strode towards the man and pulled him into a firm hug. Dorian had been present when the Creator had breathed life into Epimetheus, it was only fitting that he should receive the first female companion.

"How are you Dorian?" Epimetheus asked in his native tongue.

"I am well. Welcome to the Great Hall." Dorian said gesturing to the temple around them.

Epimetheus looked around him in awe. "It is beautiful."

The Creator led them back to the table and motioned for everyone to take their seats.

"Epimetheus, please come forward." The Creator instructed.

Dorian watched the man walk toward his Creator with confidence and trust. Once Epimetheus stood in front of him, the Creator placed his hands on his shoulders and smiled broadly at him. Dorian saw the Creator whisper to his creation, then place his forehead against the man's. Epimetheus turned and lowered himself to the ground, where he lay on his back with his eyes closed.

The Council of Immortals watched curiously as the Creator placed his hand on the man's head.

"Sleep now my son." He said gently with a small smile on his face.

With one hand on Epimetheus dark hair, he held the other hand over the man's abdomen. A beautiful light began to emanate from beneath his hand, and continued to grow brighter until the Creator stood, holding a bone in his hand.

The Council of Immortals followed the Creators every move as he laid the curved bone in the center of the table. Dorian recognized the bone as a section of Epimetheus' rib cage. He glanced over at Epimetheus, sure that a removal of this sort would have caused the man great physical pain, but Epimetheus appeared to be sleeping peacefully.

"Before you is the beginning of woman. Man must be able to recognize a piece of himself within his mate. Man must also be able to accept woman as his partner, someone to stand beside him." The Creator began his explanation. "He must be able to wrap his arm around her to show her affection as well as to offer her protection."

"Have you discussed what you would like to share with woman as she comes into being?" The Creator asked the Council of Immortals.

"We have." They replied as one.

"Charis, come forward. Your giving spirit will be perfect to begin our project." The Creator beckoned.

Charis stepped up to the Creator and bowed her head slightly. She smiled up at him and then went to place her hand on the bone in the middle of the table.

"Woman will be kind. She will be warm and comforting to her family and friends. She will be hospitable. Her soul will be soft and welcoming. Woman will be the ultimate nurturer." Charis said confidently in her soft voice. She smiled at the Creator and returned to her seat.

Caprice came forward next and placed her hand on the bone. "Woman will be capable of great love. She will be passionate. She will offer man a life filled with affection and become his life-long lover."

Once Caprice had taken her seat, Lida stepped forward and placed her hand on the bone.

"Woman will be curious. She will have a sense of humor and be able to laugh with her mate. She will be in constant pursuit of knowledge. She will be creative and inventive. Her smile will light up the room." Lida said with a grin.

"Do any of the men have something to share with our new creation before she becomes flesh and blood?" The Creator asked.

Absalom stepped forward. "Woman will be a good judge of character."

Romulus touched the rib. "Woman will be strong in mind and body."

Marcellus took his turn next. "Woman will be vulnerable where man is strong, and strong where man is vulnerable."

Rance came forward. "Woman will be intellectual."

Silas reached for the bone, his eyes on Caprice. "Woman will have great beauty."

Lucien closed his eyes and touched the rib. "Woman will be led by her heart."

Finally, Dorian leaned across the table and took his turn. "Woman will be fruitful."

The Creator held his arms open wide and took a deep breath. Light poured out of him and surrounded the rib bone. It began to levitate and a body took shape. Dorian watched in awe as woman took form within the light. As she came back to the table, she lay covered in a white gauzy material.

"She is beautiful." Epimetheus said, breaking the silence. He came forward and took her hand in his as her eyes fluttered open. She looked up at him with confusion before she relaxed and smiled.

"Pandora." The Creator called. "Rise and receive your gift."

The woman slowly stood with help from Epimetheus. She smiled at him as he helped her off the table, his hands resting on her waist.

The Creator revealed a golden sphere. It caught the light and sent sparkles around the Great Hall.

"It is breathtaking." She said in a melodic voice. "What is it?"

"This sphere was created by Absalom. I sent him to retrieve all the beings that may threaten my prefect world. I cannot allow my creations to procreate in a world where these creatures are free. I am giving this to you for safekeeping. You must never let it fall or break, you must never try to see the beings within." The Creator warned as he handed the sphere to Pandora.

"I will do as you ask my lord." Pandora said, still staring wide-eyed at the sphere.

The Creator nodded at both of his creations and took their hands in his. "Go into the world together and build your lives."

With a wave of his hand, the humans were gone and he faded away. The Council of Immortals were left in their Great Hall with the realization that they had just helped create the future.

Chapter One: Tahlia

2015

She ran through the trees with her blond hair bouncing in its pony tail behind her. Her heart was beating so hard she thought it might burst from her chest. She glanced over her shoulder to see if they were following her, and discovered they were. They would soon catch her and try to destroy her.

Ever since the day they destroyed Absalom, she had been chased by these monsters. They had never gotten this close to her. The creatures that had been released by Pandora now ran amuck through the world. For years, Tahlia had been the only one who stood between them and their devious plans.

Tahlia made a sharp turn and broke through the trees. The moonlight shone down, casting a pale glow around her. Now that she was in the open, she turned to face her attackers. Pain broke through the trees first, followed closely by Panic and Malice.

Pain resembled his name. Just looking at the little urchin hurt; he had twisted limbs and scarred flesh coving his hunched body. Panic always reminded her of a junkie; he was always flitting around. Malice was cold and dark. She had straight black hair and pale white skin; her black eyes were always filled with hatred.

Tahlia knew they just needed to touch her in order to infect her with their maladies. She kept her force field firmly in place.

"All alone. Helpless and alone." Panic sang in a taunting voice.

"Alone, but never helpless." Tahlia replied evenly.

"You don't know where you are. How will you get home? How will your family know where to look for your body?" Panic asked sardonically.

Tahlia heard the truth in his words and closed her eyes trying to push down the panic rising in her chest. She was distracted by breaking twigs as two more figures loped out of the woods.

Malice giggled with maniacal glee as Disease and Vanity made their way into the clearing. Tahlia felt her stomach turn as the smell hit her.

Disease was tall, skeletal, and covered in oozing pustules; the smell of death and decay floated in the air around him. Vanity kept her distance, clearly disgusted by her companion. It never ceased to amaze Tahlia how these creatures worked together despite their extreme differences.

They had surrounded her. Pain, Panic, and Disease were standing in front of her. Triumph was written all over their faces, but they should have known Tahlia wasn't going down without a fight.

"Vanity, your shoes are dirty." Tahlia said in mock terror.

A squeal escaped Vanity as she desperately tried to wipe the mud off her high heels. A disgusted sound came from Malice as she glared at Vanity.

Tahlia felt a small amount of joy from tormenting Vanity. She reminded her of the stereotypical cheerleader from teen movies. She was a striking beauty, and the complete opposite of Malice with her luscious blond locks and tan skin.

Tahlia didn't understand what they were waiting for. They'd been alone in this clearing for long enough. She looked carefully at each of her foes, assessing the risks of an attack. No matter what happened, she couldn't let them see her fear.

She felt a shudder run through her body. The energy gathered within her as she prepared for her attack. Tahlia closed her eyes and pushed a wave of energy out around her. As it hit the Maladies around her, they fell to the ground disoriented. She didn't have time to think, she turned and ran to the other side of the clearing and didn't stop.

Chapter Two: Nora

Nora sat at the kitchen island with her hands wrapped around a coffee mug. She had only just gotten to relax after putting her little girl to bed. There were only a few hours to go until her daughter turned four. She smiled at the memory of the day they met her. She and Kerr had looked at her beautiful face and finally knew what real love was. They had decided to name her after Romulus' son, Keiran. Little Keira had brought so much light into their lives in just a few years.

She watched the seconds tick by on the kitchen clock. The house was filled with a deafening silence that left her feeling small and lonely. Nora was consumed by her thoughts. She was worried about what lay ahead for her family. Thatcher and Romulus were expected home earlier and hadn't returned. Eric was on the campaign trail; he was up for re-election so they hadn't seen him in weeks. Dorian had been shutting himself in the library trying desperately to work out what the Creator had in store for them next. Hadley had been trying to find a way to bring her sister back. It was all Nora could do to keep everyone together and sane.

She looked at the clock again. It was late and Tahlia hadn't returned home from her evening jog. The knot in Nora's stomach was beginning to nauseate her.

Tahlia should know better than to be out after dark. Ever since they had destroyed Silas and Absalom, Tahlia had been plagued by nightmares about the evils that escaped the sphere before she appeared. Nora closed her eyes and listened, hoping she would hear Tahlia calling for her. Instead of hearing her aunt, she heard the front door bang open, echoing in the front hall.

Nora stood up so fast she knocked over the bar stool she'd been perched on. She ran around the corner to find herself face to face with a disheveled Tahlia.

"What the hell happened to you?" Nora asked in disbelief.

"It wasn't a dream this time." Tahlia said as she sank to the floor.

Nora felt her stomach clench as she realized what her aunt was telling her. They had found her.

"Why didn't you call to me?" Nora demanded.

Tahlia shook her head as she stared into Nora's eyes. "I can't risk you like that. Your family needs you."

Nora felt her chest tighten as tears sprang to her eyes. Tahlia would sacrifice herself for any of them, but she would never accept that they would all do the same.

"I need to go shower. I lost them and just kept running until I made it home. They won't find me here. Please don't tell anyone, I wouldn't want to worry them."

"It's a little late for that mom." Hadley said from the stairs.

Nora turned to find Hadley and Dorian staring at them. Hadley had her arms crossed as she glared at her mother with a mixture of concern and irritation. Dorian descended into the foyer and helped Tahlia up. He didn't say a word. He just led her to the stairs and assisted her as she climbed them.

Nora watched Hadley visibly relax once her mother was out of sight. She shrugged apologetically at her best friend.

"Just be thankful she made it home safely." Nora told her.

"Oh I am. But I wish she would stop being so stubborn." Hadley replied.

"Yeah. I don't know anyone else around here like that." Nora said with a grin.

"Who? Me?" Hadley feigned surprise.

The girls laughed as they made their way upstairs. Nora headed down the hall to the room she shared with Kerr. She opened the door quietly, trying not to wake her sleeping husband.

"Did Tahlia make it home?" Kerr's voice startled her as the door latched behind her.

"Yes. They found her. She barely escaped." Nora whispered as she climbed into bed and settled next to Kerr.

"Is she alright? Do I need to heal her?" Kerr asked as his muscles tightened slightly under her head.

"She's fine. Just exhausted. She ran the whole way. She could have called me." Nora said sounding like a sulking child.

Kerr laughed silently, wrapping his arms around her. She smiled as he kissed the top of her head.

"Oh Nora, I love you." Kerr said, his smile evident.

"Well, I can't say I blame you." Nora replied, snaking her arm around his naked abdomen.

Kerr laughed out loud. They snuggled in and fell asleep.

Chapter Three: Thatcher

Thatcher watched as the people walked up and down the street. He wasn't sure what he was waiting for, but he knew he'd recognize it when it appeared. He had spent the last few years tracking down the effects of the negative energy released into the world after Absalom was killed.

The day he destroyed his ancestor Thatcher had absorbed all the abilities Absalom had stolen from the descendants he had murdered. But they discovered a few short months later that they hadn't just released the abilities. They had released the evil.

The world had become a terrifying place. Thatcher often felt like he and the other Evolved were part of a supernatural cleanup crew. They had been traveling the world whenever an area displayed a spike in negative energy.

He and Romulus had made this trip to Chicago a few weeks ago. They had been working tirelessly to find and calm the people who appeared to be infected with Absalom's negativity. Both Romulus and Kerr had the ability to incite emotions in others; but they could only counter an emotion someone was already feeling. If someone was angry, they could calm them. If someone was depressed, they could help them dig out of the depths of despair. It was the only way they were able to nullify the evil they had encountered.

Romulus came up beside him and cast a sidelong glance at Thatcher. This had become their pattern. They split up, did their rounds, then came back to make sure the other was alright.

"Did you find him?" Thatcher asked.

Romulus shook his head. "No. But he's here. Lurking. Waiting for the next girl."

Thatcher felt his stomach turn as he thought about the condition they had found the last girl in. They had been tracking a man who abducted women from Millennium Park. He took them and did disgusting things to them before dumping their bodies on the Red Line train. The girls usually disappeared in the afternoon, and would reappear the next morning.

Thatcher caught the sound as though the world had gone silent. A muffled cry to his left. With his heart pounding in his chest, he turned and made his way towards the sound. Romulus wordlessly followed, understanding that Thatcher would fill him in when it was time. He walked down the street and came to an alley. Thatcher knew he needed to gain a better perspective, so he leapt into the air. He usually only flew when he wanted to feel close to Malcolm, but he knew this was the only way to see. Careful to stay near the building to avoid being noticed, he peered around until he saw the man struggling to pull a woman off the street.

Thatcher came back to the ground and motioned for Romulus to follow him. "He's just around the corner. I don't know where he's taking her, but she's putting up a fight. That should slow him down."

They made it around the building in time to see the woman twist out of his grasp and stumble as she tried to run. He must have drugged her. Romulus' face was tight, his mouth drawn in a thin line. It was clear that he was struggling to control the emotions of this predator. The man stood staring at them, but Thatcher could see he was going to fight anything Romulus threw at him.

"You're going to be alright." Thatcher said soothingly as he approached the young woman on the ground.

"I can't move my legs." She answered in terror.

"I need you to stay as calm as possible. Here's my cell phone. Call 911." Thatcher replied as he handed her the burner phone.

He turned to Romulus to ask if he could help, but found the Old Immortal shaking as he attempted to maintain control.

"This man doesn't feel anything. I can only catch bits of emotion. None of them are strong enough to hold him." Romulus said through gritted teeth.

This wasn't a result of Absalom's negative energy; this was something else entirely. He felt someone watching them from the shadow of the alley. Thatcher whipped around to see a tall thin man standing at the edge of the darkness. Thinking quickly, Thatcher lunged at the man who had attacked the woman. It broke the connection Romulus had created, but gave Thatcher the advantage. He landed on top of the man, and pulled his arm back. He felt his fist connect with the man's jaw and heard a sickening crack. A hand gripped him from behind, he felt a surge of anger fill him and punched the man again. As he pulled back to take another swing, Romulus caught his arm.

"Thatcher, we need to leave. There was another man here, one that we cannot fight. The police will be here soon. The woman will be alright. We should go unless you want to spend the rest of the day down at the precinct." Romulus said to him.

Thatcher closed his eyes and took a deep breath. He knew Romulus was right, but he couldn't calm the rage that tightened his chest. The man lying underneath him was a monster. He had a darkness in him that was inhuman. Thatcher didn't think he should live. He represented everything they were trying to eradicate from the world.

"Why was it so hard for you to influence his emotions?" Thatcher asked.

Romulus shrugged. "It was strange. He wasn't feeling anything. All I could sense was darkness and anger. It was as though all he had inside him was fury. If there is no opposite emotion present, I can't counter it."

The two stood against the building, watching the man warily. Thatcher was ready to strike again if the man so much as took a deep breath.

It didn't take long before the alley was flooded with police officers. Thatcher and Romulus disappeared in the commotion.

Chapter Four: Kerr

Kerr woke to the sound of the hair dryer as Nora got herself ready for the day. He smiled to himself and lay with is eyes closed for a few moments. They had a big day planned for Keira's fourth birthday. Everyone was supposed to be home.

There had not been much time to be together since Absalom died. When Nora brought Thatcher back from the battle, Kerr had experienced a vision that left him wondering what would be next. Kerr allowed himself to relive the vision as he did every morning to keep it fresh in his mind.

A woman was kneading dough near a window. The room was simple, the walls appeared to be made of clay. Kerr watched the woman for a moment before he wandered to another window to take a closer look at the scenery. There was a breathtaking view of the ocean, and the hut appeared to be surrounded by others like it. He was alerted to the arrival of a man as the woman addressed him.

"Epimetheus! Welcome home!" She said with a smile on her face.

"Hello my love. How has the day been?" Epimetheus asked.

"It has been as fair a day as any." The woman replied.

Kerr watched as Epimetheus kissed the woman on her forehead and embraced her. He became rigid in her embrace as he noticed something out of place.

"Pandora, why is the sphere out in the open?" Epimetheus asked with great concern.

"I was just looking at it." Pandora replied.

Kerr looked over at a chair in the corner and saw a beautiful object. It was gold and glowing, pulsing with an ethereal light. He couldn't take his eyes off it.

"You know we are to protect it, we are not to play with it." Epimetheus scolded.

"I know. I was only interested in the beings inside. It seems cruel to keep them locked away." Pandora said in a troubled tone.

"We must trust that the Creator knows what is best." Epimetheus said as he carefully picked up the glowing golden sphere.

Pandora reached for it and snatched it from Epimetheus' hands. Kerr heard the sharp intake of breath as Epimetheus saw how carelessly his mate handled the precious sphere. Pandora held it up to her eye as though trying to peer in.

"Sometimes I think I can hear them speaking to me. They speak to me in dreams. Their whispers tell me the Creator is trying to keep us from being like him. I have spoken with one of the Immortals, he has confirmed this suspicion." Pandora said as if in a trance.

"That is absurd. The Creator only has our best interests in mind. We are his children, he made us. He would never do something that would hurt us. Who is the Immortal you have spoken with?" Epimetheus asked in a steady voice.

Pandora shrugged her shoulders and continued to examine the sphere. Kerr knew Hadley had discovered that Tahlia *was* born of the sphere, but none of them had been told how it had happened. He had a feeling he was about to find out.

"I think it best we put it away." Epimetheus told his wife.

"But I can hear them." Pandora replied as though in a trance. "They want to come out."

Kerr watched in horror as Pandora simply let the sphere fall from her hands. He heard Epimetheus scream and saw him fall helplessly to his knees.

Instead of hitting the floor, the sphere stopped inches above the ground and began to shake. Dark cracks began appearing and black smoke began to snake its way out of each fissure. Suddenly, it shattered as though something inside exploded.

Each fragment of the sphere began to take the shape of some creature but they whooshed away before becoming corporeal. Kerr felt the fear, anger, pain, and confusion as each strange malady passed by and through him during its *escape. He saw Pandora fall to her knees next to her husband, wailing in fear and regret.*

When all the dark smoky figures had gone, Kerr sank to the ground in relief. It was over. But there was one piece of the sphere remaining on the floor. A curious smell began to fill the air that reminded Kerr of the first blooms of spring. Golden light filled the room, growing so intense that Kerr had to shield his eyes.

When he opened them again, Tahlia stood in front of him. She was bathed in the golden light, she was wearing a dress that appeared to have been made from the light. Kerr let out the breath he had been holding and watched as Tahlia walked toward the couple cowering in the corner.

"Pandora, you have broken the trust the Creator had placed in you. You have released all the Maladies back into the world. They are now free to do as they please. I am the final piece of the sphere. I am Elpis. The spirit of hope." Tahlia told her.

Pandora whimpered quietly, nodding her head.

"Because of your betrayal, I have been asked to tell you that humankind will no longer be able to speak with the Creator face to face. You will never again be able to hold assembly with the Creator or the Council of Immortals. This will be your last encounter with one of our kind." *Tahlia told them in a gentle but stern voice that Kerr was familiar with.*

The light grew more intense until Tahlia was gone. Kerr began to fade away as Pandora and Epimetheus clung to each other and cried.

Nora came out of the bathroom and smiled at Kerr. She finished getting dressed and turned to face him again.

"You should get your lazy self out of bed. We've got a little girl to spoil!" Nora said with a giggle.

"I know. I was just thinking." Kerr said quietly.

"Were you thinking about your vision again?" Nora asked as she sat on the edge of the bed.

Kerr nodded. "Every morning. It was the first full vision I had of the past. I need to know why."

Nora put her hand on his shoulder and leaned over until she was nose to nose with Kerr.

"We've been over this a million times. Absalom had absorbed all the evil of the world. When he died, it had nowhere to go, just like when the sphere shattered. Dorian is searching to see if there is more to it than that." Nora said soothingly as she gave Kerr a quick kiss.

Kerr nodded and made his way to the bathroom. He knew she was right, but he had a nagging feeling that there was more to it than that. He felt he was missing some important detail that would help them as they fought the evil that Absalom had held within him.

Chapter Five: Hadley

Hadley leaned her head against the window in the sitting room. After the commotion of the night before, she was anxious for Thatcher to return. She closed her eyes and drew in a deep breath.

The years without Whitley had only been bearable because of her family. She had grown much closer to her mother, and the idea that those evil creatures had finally caught up with her was almost too much for her to process. The nightmares her mother had been having had been terrifying just to hear about. But the thought of those monsters being close enough to touch her mom left a sick feeling in the pit of her stomach.

If they were willing to get that close to her mother, what would stop them from attacking the rest of her family? Thatcher was always off on missions with Romulus or Kerr. Anything could happen to any of them. She couldn't bear losing anyone else.

She turned her thoughts to her research. Hadley had been diving head first into the library trying to find any loophole that would bring her sister back to her. So far she had not found anything that indicated that was possible. But she knew her sister was still there, waiting. Whitley had become part of her, she talked to her every night in her dreams. Whitley had accepted her decision and continued to tell her to stop looking for a way to bring her back into the real world. But she couldn't.

Her life without Whitley felt empty. Based on the prophecy she should feel whole; the two had been reunited. But Whitley wasn't just a part of her, Whitley was her own person. There were parts of her twin that she would never be, and she would not lose those attributes if she didn't have to.

A knock at the door startled Hadley from her thoughts. She looked up to see her mother peeking into the room. Hadley got up quickly and rushed to hug her mother.

"Mom, I'm so glad you're alright." Hadley said into her mother's shoulder.

"I can take care of myself" Tahlia said trying to reassure her, but Hadley pulled away and shook her head.

"No. You can't do that. You don't get to do that anymore. You have us. None of us are willing to let you sacrifice yourself to protect us. So knock it off." Hadley had her arms crossed and her brows furrowed.

"But they're my demons. Not yours." Tahlia replied.

"You're wrong. They represent the very thing we have been spending all these years trying to eradicate from the world. The Evolved were created to destroy these threats and bring the world into the next era. If you don't let us do that, you're going against the Creator." Hadley held her arms rigid, her hands in fists at her sides.

Tahlia stared open-mouthed at Hadley. She knew her mother was probably upset by her outburst, but she needed to make Tahlia understand that she didn't need protecting anymore.

The door opened wide and a little girl with deep auburn curls came bounding in, running straight for Tahlia. Hadley smiled as Keira leapt into Tahlia's arms.

"Hello sweetheart!" Tahlia exclaimed as she hugged Keira tightly.

"Hi Lia! Do you know what today is?" The little girl asked seriously.

"Hmmm, I think it's Friday." Tahlia replied with a sly grin.

As Keira giggled her green eyes lit up and her small freckled nose crinkled.

"I know what day it is." Hadley whispered conspiratorially to her pseudo-niece.

Keira squealed and leaned over reaching for Hadley. She gladly took the little girl from Tahlia.

"Happy birthday little one." Hadley whispered into Keira's curls.

Nora nodded and turned to follow her husband and daughter into the kitchen.

Chapter Six: Dorian

Dorian sat in the library staring at the shelves of books before him. He was lost in thought, unsure of where to turn next. He had been over each book at least twice since the day Kerr had his vision. He was not sure why Kerr was given that particular vision or if it truly had any significant meaning to the future of the Old Immortals and the Evolved. But he had promised Kerr he would look into it.

He scratched his well-trimmed beard and sighed through his nose. So far the only connection he could find was the nightmares, and now physical appearance, involving the evils released before Tahlia. There was little known about where the Maladies had come from. All he could remember was that Absalom had found the purest evils and the Creator had trapped them in the sphere. But they had never asked where they came from or how Absalom had managed to find them.

Considering how Absalom turned out, Dorian couldn't help but think that his brother had somehow been changed even then.

According to the History of the Old Immortals, Absalom had been a bad seed from the beginning. Try as he might, Dorian couldn't remember if there had ever been a time when his brother had been on their side. He recalled the incidents that had gotten his brother into trouble; volcanoes, hot springs, wildfires. But he didn't want to believe that Absalom had always been evil. Could finding these evil beings have set the events in motion that led to his corruption? Could he have been corrupted even then? No. Dorian refused to believe all those years ago, at the very beginning, that even then his brother was plotting against them.

He finished writing his notes and put his tablet away. He felt someone watching him and turned to see Keira peering above the back of the couch. He smiled at her and held his arms open.

"Happy birthday little one!" He said as he enveloped her in a hug.

Keira sat on his lap and reached up to touch his face; stroking his beard. He knew she could sense his frustration because this was how she always tried to calm him when he was on edge.

"Papa, everything will be alright." Keira said soothingly.

Dorian gave her a perplexed look as he tried to determine how much she truly knew about her world. The child was wise beyond her years but he wanted to protect her for as long as possible.

"I know sweet pea. I just need to reassure everyone else." He whispered conspiratorially and touched the tip of her nose.

She grinned and leaned back into his arms. This was their morning tradition. Keira would come into the library, reminding him for all the world of her mother, and climb up into his lap for a morning chat. He knew from the day she was born that she would be a force to be reckoned with. The daughter of two strong-willed descendants of an ancient race, she had double the ability coursing through her body and only time would tell how it would manifest.

Dorian knew that no matter who Keira became, she would be protected from the Maladies and taught the history of her family. But he also knew that his granddaughter was described as the hope of the future. Was she in more danger than they thought because of her connection to the spirit of hope?

"Papa, I had a bad dream last night." Keira said quietly.

"Oh did you? Well, tell me all about it sweetheart." Dorian said seriously.

Keira bit her lip for a moment before launching into the story that would change the direction of Dorian's research.

"Well, I was in the middle of a field with trees around me. Big trees. It was dark and

I was scared. Then Lia ran out of the trees." Keira paused.

Dorian felt the hair on the back of his neck stand up as he recognized the story Tahlia had told him. "What happened then Keira?"

"I don't want to say. I didn't like it." She said with a serious tone and strained face.

"Ok. Well, if you can't tell me about your bad dreams how can I help you see there's nothing to fear?" Dorian asked her, trying not to press her.

Keira nodded, this made sense to her; she was looking for reassurance that it had just been a dream and not to be scared. Her little face relaxed and she closed her eyes as though trying to remember.

"Lia stopped and turned around. I tried to yell to her that there was someone there, but she couldn't hear me. The others came through the trees and started walking towards her. One of them looked like he was hurt, but not the kind of hurt you can fix. Another looked like everything scared him, and the last one looked like she hated everyone." Keira paused, waiting for reassurance.

"Sounds scary. What happened next?" Dorian asked as he shifted in the chair until he was facing her.

"It was scary. But Lia wasn't scared. She just talked to them. Then two more scary people came out. One was a girl, she was kinda pretty, but not in a nice way. The other one...." Keira shuddered involuntary. "He was yucky. He smelled and needed to see a doctor."

"With so many bad people around, what did Tahlia do?" Dorian asked carefully.

"Nothing. She just stood there. But I could tell she was getting scared. I thought maybe a hug would help. So I went up beside her and wrapped my arms around her legs. I felt her shaking and wanted to give her some of my brave like you always do if I'm scared."

Dorian nodded, he was very interested in where this was going. Somehow, little Keira had been present but unseen in the clearing with Tahlia.

"Is there more?" He asked.

Keira nodded. "That's the crazy part Papa. I was hugging Lia and it felt like she was trying to use her magic and couldn't. So I gave her some of mine."

Dorian froze for a moment before stroking her back to provide some comfort. Keira always referred to their abilities as 'magic'. He blamed fairy tales and Disney, but knew she wasn't quite old enough to understand how much deeper their abilities ran than magic beans and fairy godmothers.

"Oh. I didn't know you had magic little one." Dorian said curiously.

"Neither did I. But it was just a bad dream. So I thought I could do anything. I just imagined my magic going into her legs and helping her get away from the scary people. And it did. She had more than enough magic to knock those bad guys on their butts." Keira said with a smug smile.

"Wow. What a fascinating dream." Dorian told her. "Have you ever had a dream like that before?"

Keira shook her head seriously. Then her bright green eyes widened as she jumped off Dorians lap.

"I smell pancakes!" She called over her shoulder as she bounded out of the room at break-neck speed.

Dorian grabbed his tablet and quickly made more notes so he wouldn't forget everything Keira had just told him.

Chapter Seven: Nora

Nora smiled to herself as she watched Kerr make breakfast for the family. He had made it a tradition to make Keira her favorite breakfast on her birthday. He started mixing the ingredients for the pancakes. Keira giggled uncontrollably when he dropped an egg on the floor and he smiled and kissed her forehead.

Nora glanced at the clock on the wall and wondered when Thatcher and Romulus would call for her to come get them. They had been able to save money on travel with Nora's gift, and she loved being the person they depended on when they wanted to come home.

Nora went down the hallway to see how Dorian was doing but stopped when she heard Tahlia speaking to him. They were discussing what had happened to Tahlia the night before, but Dorian kept bringing Keira up. He told Tahlia about a dream Keira had, a dream that indicated she had been there during the failed attack on Tahlia. After a few minutes, she decided she had heard enough and barged into the library without knocking.

"And when were you going to tell me about this?" Nora asked, barely controlling her anger.

"Nora!" Tahlia exclaimed. "Dorian only just told me. Keira told him this morning. We were going to tell you."

Nora calmed down a bit and tried to process what she'd just overheard. Her daughter was projecting herself into other places while she slept. Her little, four-year-old daughter was appearing in a field in the middle of nowhere, 'giving' her power to someone else. How could she possibly protect her if she was involuntarily travelling to God knows where?

Nora sank down onto the oversized chair she'd spent so much time in over the years. She buried her face in her hands. Dorian knelt in front of her and took her hands in his.

"Nora, we will figure it out. This doesn't change anything. Tahlia didn't know she was there. The Maladies thought Tahlia was alone. They couldn't sense Keira either. If anything this gives us a better idea of what to expect as Keira gets older. We know more about what her gifts may be."

Nora knew he was right. It sounded like her abilities were going to be amazing. She could travel unseen but still have an effect on her surroundings. She could share her abilities with others. But it's a mother's job to worry about her child. And her concern was strong regarding this new development.

"How did it feel when she gave you her power Tahlia?" Nora asked quietly.

"I didn't know that was what was happening at the time, but I'd only been able to produce a shield until that moment. Then I suddenly knew I could do it. I felt the power pulsing through me. I knew it was there, and I used it. I honestly didn't think I had that much power left in me. And now I know I probably don't." Tahlia said. "Keira saved my life. I don't know how she knew I would need her, but she was there when I needed her most."

Nora felt a tear fall down her cheek. Her little girl had saved the only mother Nora had ever known. Keira was showing them just how special she was.

"We can't tell her it was real. Not yet." Nora told them firmly. "Once she's in bed tonight we can have a meeting and tell everyone else."

Dorian and Tahlia agreed.

As she was about to get up and head back into the kitchen she heard and felt the distress in Thatcher's voice screaming in her head.

"I have to go." Nora said suddenly. "I need Hadley with me. It's not good."

Dorian looked at her with concern. She didn't have time to explain. She ran out of the library in search of Hadley.

She found Hadley playing a clapping game with Keira in the kitchen. She grabbed her arm and pulled her close.

"It's Thatcher. We need to go. Now." She whispered.

The look in Hadley's eyes told her she understood and took her hand without hesitation.

"I'll be back soon baby." Nora told Keira as she blew her a kiss and disappeared.

They rematerialized on a rooftop in Chicago. She whirled around looking for Thatcher and Romulus. She didn't see them anywhere.

This had been where the call was coming from. She knew it. Where were they?

"Nora?" Hadley asked with concern.

"I know Had. Something is off." Nora took Hadley's hand and made them invisible to anyone who may stumble upon them.

They started looking around for a door but couldn't find one. There was only one thing

Hadley nodded. "I'm staying here. I need to find Thatcher."

Nora started to respond but was cut off when Romulus grabbed her arm. She looked at him with tears in her eyes. She felt so helpless.

"Can't leave. Bring Kerr."

Nora understood his plea and disappeared in an instant.

She materialized in the kitchen again to the stunned, pancake filled faces of her family. She realized she was covered in blood from trying to wake Romulus, Kerr was at her side in an instant.

She looked at her little girl covered in syrup and tried to give them a reassuring smile as she disappeared with Kerr.

Chapter Eight: Kerr

When Kerr saw Romulus his stomach fell. He was much paler than he usually was and the bleeding didn't seem to be slowing down. He knew this didn't mean he would die, only the Evolved could kill an Old Immortal.

Kerr rushed forward to begin the healing process. He fell to his knees next to his ancestor and placed a hand on his forehead. He focused on the pain and began willing it to leave Romulus' body. The now familiar green light began to wind its way around the man in front of him. To his horror, he was filled with fragmented memories of the events that left Romulus bleeding in the alley.

When the healing light dissipated, Romulus looked at Kerr sadly. Kerr couldn't believe what he had seen; he wouldn't believe it.

"No." Kerr said firmly to Romulus.

"What?" Hadley demanded, panic evident in her voice.

"It's true Kerr. I don't know how or why but it's true. We need to find him." Romulus told him, ignoring Hadley's question.

Kerr shook his head, he was lost. He had seen Thatcher attacking Romulus. A vicious, maniacal attack that only stopped when Thatcher thought he had killed Romulus. The worst part of it all is exactly how close he had been to killing Romulus. Kerr knew Thatcher was not that person. He knew Thatcher would not have done something that heinous under normal circumstances.

But what had caused him to attack the gentle Old Immortal?

"Kerr. You have to tell us what's going on." Nora told him, placing a hand on his arm.

Kerr looked apologetically at his wife and Hadley.

"It was Thatcher. He did this." Kerr said in a voice barely above a whisper.

"No way!" Hadley said breathlessly. "He would never. I don't believe it."

Nora looked troubled by this development. Kerr knew this would not be received well, but he wasn't mistaken. Thatcher had attacked Romulus.

"It was strange. We caught the guy who was killing women. I couldn't counter his emotions when we confronted him. Thatcher lunged at him and sucker punched him. Then, he began beating him mercilessly after another man ran past and grabbed at his back, but he stopped when I took hold of his arm and told him to stop." Romulus told them.

"What happened after that?" Nora asked gently.

"We waited in the alley for the police to come because we couldn't leave until we were sure he had been taken into custody. The other man had fled just after touching

Thatcher. Once the police arrived we left, we didn't want to be there for questioning. We were going to call for you Nora, but when we got to the alley here it was almost like Thatcher was fighting with himself." Romulus closed his eyes.

"He seemed irrational. He yelled at people for looking at him. When I told him to relax he lost it. He was using his abilities against me. Every swipe of his hand caused my skin to rip open violently. I begged him to stop." Romulus was crying as he recounted what happened to him.

"I told him he was killing me. I fell to my knees in front of him and put my head down, waiting for the final blow. But it didn't come. Instead I heard him say, 'Oh God.' I looked up at him in time to see him launch into the air. He was almost out of sight when I heard a tortured scream for you, Nora. That was when I knew that the real Thatcher was fighting with whatever was going on inside his mind." Romulus buried his face in his hands and cried.

Kerr didn't know what to say. He didn't know what would make any of it better for Romulus or Hadley. He glanced at Hadley and saw how heartbroken she looked after hearing what Thatcher had done.

"That explains why the call led me to the top of that building." Nora said dumfounded.

"So what do you think happened to him?" Hadley asked with concern.

"I hate to say it, but the man who touched him, I've seen him before. He was one of the Maladies. I'd asked Thatcher how he felt after the contact, but he said he was alright. It didn't hit him until a little later." Romulus told them.

Kerr didn't know what to think but he knew they had to find Thatcher. They couldn't let him run around when he was a danger to himself and others. He knew that when Thatcher recovered from whatever this was he would feel terrible about what happened with Romulus, he could only imagine how

much worse he would feel if he hurt anyone
else.

Chapter Nine: Tahlia

Tahlia smiled at Keira as she slept on the couch where she had been patiently waiting for the family to return. Eric had arrived shortly after the Evolved left. He found her sitting with Dorian and Keira talking about all the things she hoped to receive for her birthday.

Tahlia was preoccupied with worry as they had no connection to the Evolved or Romulus. She knew that for them to be gone this long something was terribly wrong. When Nora had returned covered in blood to take Kerr back with her Tahlia knew there was something serious going on.

"Lia, calm down." Eric said placing a hand on her knee to still her nervous bouncing.

"I can't. They may be special, but they're still so young. Anyone who had lost enough blood to cover Nora like that had to have been close to death. If it was Thatcher..." Her voice caught as she thought of her daughter and everything she had been through over the last five years.

"Kerr is with them. I'm certain they would have returned if they hadn't been able to save whoever was injured. They are probably working together to stop whoever harmed them." Dorian told her calmly.

Tahlia didn't know how he could sit there so calmly. He didn't seem to be concerned for the safety of the Evolved at all. She knew she shouldn't be worried either but she had embraced all of those kids as though they were her own. She had lost one of her daughters because of the battles they had to fight. She knew she would not be calm until her family was back home.

"No. Don't!" Keira whimpered in her sleep.

Tahlia and Dorian were instantly at attention as they exchanged a nervous look. There was no telling if Keira was dreaming or experiencing the same projection she had with Tahlia the night before.

"What's going on?" Eric asked uneasily.

"Shhh!" Tahlia told him as Keira began to speak again.

"Uncle Thatcher, can't you hear me? Don't do that." Keira demanded in her little voice.

Tahlia grew more concerned at the strain she saw in Keira's face. She didn't know what the little girl was seeing but she looked very anxious even in her sleep.

"Should we wake her?" Dorian asked in alarm.

Before Tahlia could answer the little girl screamed. She had heard Keira scream with delight, she had heard her scream with excitement, but she had never heard her scream in terror. This was terror; her scream tore through the sitting room and sent chills down Tahlia's back.

Without hesitation, Dorian reached forward and gently shook his granddaughter. He shook a little harder when she wouldn't wake. He looked to Tahlia in a panic when the screaming stopped but Keira still hadn't awoken.

"Tahlia we need to do something!" Dorian said in anguish, barely keeping himself from shouting.

"Keira, sweetie, we need you to wake up." Tahlia said as she rubbed the girl's cheek.

Keira let out a small moan and her eyes fluttered open. When she caught sight of Dorian she threw her arms around his neck and cried into his shoulder.

"Oh Papa. Thatcher needs us. He's not bad. He's not bad. Right? He wouldn't hurt anyone." Keira sobbed loudly.

Eric grabbed Tahlia and pulled her to the side.

"You need to tell me what's going on. What can I do?" Eric begged as he looked down at Keira.

"We don't really know yet Eric. This morning she told Dorian about a dream she had last night. A dream that told us she had transported herself to my side in her sleep. I was confronted by the Maladies last night;

70

in person." Tahlia held up a hand to stop Eric from scolding her.

"I was out for a jog and didn't make it home before dark. The found me and I was surrounded. But I suddenly felt strong enough to fight them off and I did. As it turns out, I was only strong enough because of Keira. I didn't see her. I didn't know she was there at all until she perfectly described the entire situation to Dorian."

Eric gave her an appraising look before nodding once and turning his attention back to Keira and Dorian. They would discuss this later.

Tahlia crouched down next to them and kissed Keira gently on the head.

"Honey can you tell us what you saw?" Tahlia asked carefully.

"Why? It was just a bad dream." Keira told her quietly. It was clear the little girl didn't want to recount what she witnessed.

Tahlia and Dorian exchanged a look. They had promised Nora they wouldn't tell Keira

71

that her dreams were real. But they had to know what had happened to terrify the little girl so much.

"Keira, you know how sometimes grandpa and daddy know things before they happen or can see things someone has done?" Tahlia asked.

Keira nodded her head with tears in her eyes. "And mommy can go places without using a car."

"That's right sweetheart. Well, because you are their little girl, you are going to be able to do some special things too. Do you remember telling me about your dream last night?" Dorian asked.

Keira nodded her head again and glanced at Tahlia.

Tahlia smiled at her. "You helped me for real Keira. You helped me get away from those bad guys."

Keira's eyes widened in surprise as she realized what Tahlia was telling her.

"So when I sleep I can see you guys? And I can help. But I couldn't help Thatcher." She said sadly.

Dorian furrowed his brow. Tahlia knew they had to find out what happened if they had any hope of helping Thatcher.

"Keira, what happened to Thatcher?" Tahlia asked urgently.

"He was on top of a building. He was crying. He ripped his shirt off 'cuz it had blood on it. He went to the edge and looked down. I told him not to. But he wouldn't listen. A man appeared behind him and yelled at him to jump." Keira cried at the memory.

"Thatcher recognized the man and looked scared. All Thatcher did was lift his hand and the man fell. When he tried to get up, Thatcher....." She bit her lip as tears fell down her cheeks. "He threw him. Thatcher yelled and threw him from the building. I screamed. I think Thatcher heard me scream because he turned and looked at me.

I screamed 'cuz I thought he killed that man. But then the man came back."

Dorian and Tahlia looked at each other in alarm. Something was definitely off if Thatcher was using the abilities he had gotten from Absalom to keep someone away from him. Tahlia knew how much he struggled with using them at all because of how they had been obtained in the first place.

"What do you mean the man came back?" Tahlia asked Keira.

"He just showed up on the edge, like nothing happened." Keira whispered.

"Did you know the man?" Dorian asked.

She shook her head.

"What did the man look like?" Tahlia asked gently.

"He looked a lot like Uncle Thatcher. Bright red hair and a red beard." Keira replied.

She looked between them for a moment before bursting into tears and burying her face in Dorians shoulder again. Tahlia and Dorian exchanged a look of concern; the only man who could incite that reaction from Thatcher would be Absalom.

Tahlia closed her eyes and silently prayed for the safety of the Evolved. She knew they would be searching for Thatcher if he wasn't with them. For now, they could only wait and hope they all returned safely.

Chapter Ten: Hadley

When Hadley heard what Thatcher had done she felt as though she'd been punched in the stomach. How could he hurt Romulus? He must have been possessed or something. Romulus said the man who touched him was one of the Maladies. As soon as the thought entered her mind she began to realize she may be grasping at straws but if she'd learned anything, it was that anything was possible.

"You guys, do you think Thatcher could have been possessed by the Malady or something? Is that a real thing?" Hadley asked feeling a little foolish.

Romulus looked at her in confusion then tried to stand. Kerr and Nora helped him up and carefully stepped away once he was upright.

"In a sense, yes. But not in the way the movies would have us believe. Not that we have time for a history lesson, but it's better if you understand what's going on before we go charging after Thatcher." Romulus said in a strained voice as he struggled to maintain his balance.

"We need Tahlia." Kerr said suddenly.

"My mom? Why? What does she have to do with this?" Hadley asked.

"We need her to put the light back into Thatcher's heart." Romulus said simply.

"Oh. Right. Why didn't I think of that?" Hadley replied sarcastically. "You think you could clue those of us in who don't have special mind reading powers?"

Hadley could tell Romulus wasn't going to waste any time before beginning the search for Thatcher. She couldn't have supported that feeling more if she tried, but she needed to understand why Thatcher had suddenly lost his mind.

"It's Rage. One of the Maladies that was released into the world before your mother. Rage must have been the Malady who touched Thatcher today. He must be able to infect him by touching him. I wondered if this was how they were infecting people. He is stronger than an average human so he is able to fight off the anger inside him, giving him moments of clarity, one of which saved my life." Romulus told them.

"We'll be back." Nora grabbed Romulus' arm and disappeared.

Hadley paced back and forth for a few moments as she thought about the implications of what Romulus had told them. She knew it meant two things; one was that Thatcher wasn't completely in control of his own body and the other was that there was a physical embodiment of evil wreaking havoc in Chicago.

Nora rematerialized in the alley with Tahlia, they had left Romulus behind. Nora shot Tahlia an angry look and went to stand by Kerr with her arms crossed. Hadley didn't have time to worry about what had happened to leave Nora so irritated with Tahlia.

"We need to find Thatcher. Now." Tahlia said firmly as she headed to the mouth of the alley.

"I can't sense him at all." Nora told them.

"That's not good. That means the anger has consumed him. There may not be any of Thatcher left to sense." Tahlia told them gravely.

"What? Mom, I can't handle not knowing. Can he come back from this?" Hadley was terrified.

Tahlia came to stand next to her and placed a hand on her shoulder. "I don't know. He's alive, we just can't find him with Nora's ability if he's consumed by rage."

Hadley nodded her head and looked to Nora. She gave her a questioning look and Nora shook her head at her. Hadley knew she would find out what happened later.

"Well, what do we do now?" Kerr asked.

"Nora, you need to keep trying to sense him. If he was able to stop himself from killing Romulus he may be able to gain control sometimes." Tahlia told her.

"We're going to the top of that building. That's where Keira saw them." Tahlia said as she pointed up at a red building.

Hadley looked confused. "What do you mean where Keira saw them?"

"We'll explain later, just grab hold of Nora. Be ready for a fight." Tahlia instructed.

In the blink of an eye they were on top of the red building her mother had pointed to. As soon as they arrived she heard a voice. She made out the sound of Thatcher shouting at someone. He would pause for a few moments then yell again. She couldn't hear anyone but Thatcher so she didn't know who he was talking to.

She peaked around the corner and saw Thatcher was alone on the rooftop. There was no one to shout at, but there he stood, yelling at thin air.

Hadley started to take a step forward but was stopped by Kerr's hand on her shoulder. She tried to shrug him off but when he wouldn't budge she sent a small shock to his hand.

"Ouch! Hadley!" Kerr said shaking his hand around.

When she looked at Kerr she realized that she had never used her abilities against him. He looked mad but he was trying to stay quiet to avoid scaring Thatcher.

"He is violent you idiot. I don't care if he's your boyfriend. He nearly killed Romulus. It would take less to kill you. Don't be stupid. This isn't a movie, 'true loves kiss' isn't going to save the day." Kerr said angrily.

Hadley glared at him, she knew he was right but she didn't want Thatcher to get away. She thought if she could make him see that he was being manipulated by evil that everything would be alright.

Before Hadley could say anything in return, her mother took off running to Thatcher and Nora appeared behind him. Hadley did the only thing she could think of and threw a shield up to contain Thatcher so he wouldn't run when he realized they'd surrounded him.

Kerr was concentrating very hard next to her and she knew he was trying to bring out any calm he could grasp amidst the anger that had infected Thatcher. Hadley saw her mother slow to a walk in front of Thatcher as he eyed her warily. Hadley took a few steps forward to hear the exchange.

"What are you doing here Tahlia?" Thatcher asked, his voice deeper than usual.

"We're here to help you Thatcher." Tahlia told him evenly.

"Help me? That's rich. What are you going to do? Shield me from a mosquito?" Thatcher asked bitterly.

"No. Although you're right, that's all I'm good for these days. But, I do have a few other tricks up my sleeve. I need you to let me help you calm down." Tahlia told him.

Thatcher sneered at her as she took another step forward. He balled his hands into fists at his sides. Hadley could practically see the anger rolling off him as he watched Tahlia approach. His face softened slightly for a moment and he spoke to her.

"Tahlia, please don't do this. I don't want to hurt you. I killed Romulus. I'm just like him!" He yelled as he pointed behind Tahlia.

Hadley saw no one. She didn't know who he thought was there.

"I don't know how he's here. But he's back. He killed our families, he killed Malcolm!" Thatcher said as he fought to maintain control.

A shiver shot through her as Hadley realized who he thought was there. No wonder he couldn't maintain control of his anger, he was face to face with Absalom again.

Chapter Eleven: Thatcher

He couldn't believe Tahlia was coming between him and Absalom. Not only was she interrupting his fight, she was putting herself in danger. He felt Nora behind him and saw Hadley and Kerr further behind Tahlia.

He was so confused. They acted as though Absalom wasn't even there. He had to get them out of there. The closer Tahlia came the angrier he got.

"Get. Out. Of. Here." Thatcher said through gritted teeth. "I can handle him!"

"Oh you can handle me can you? Obviously you didn't handle me well enough the first time." Absalom hurled the words at him like the fireballs he liked to use.

"Shut-up!" Thatcher yelled grabbing his head.

Hadley took another step toward him and he was momentarily distracted by her presence. He felt the tightness in his chest as she came closer. The fury he felt was struggling to keep the concern he felt at bay.

"Get the hell out of here." Thatcher threw at Hadley. "I don't want you here."

Hadley looked hurt but determined, he knew she wouldn't leave.

"Maybe I should get rid of her for you." Absalom said as he made his way to Hadley. "I'll start with her, then go find that sweet little girl you're all so fond of. I'll raise her like I did Malcolm. One day, she'll kill you all."

"Stay away from my family. He's coming Hadley, you need to leave." Thatcher screamed at Hadley.

Why didn't she leave? Why didn't Tahlia try to stop Absalom from touching her daughter? Thatcher decided now was the time to act. He started toward Hadley but found he couldn't move.

"Drop the shield Hadley! He's going to kill you. You have to let me out!" Thatcher yelled desperately. He pushed as hard as he could and shattered the invisible shield she had placed around him.

Nora grabbed his shirt and he whirled around and hit her with a burst of energy that sent her flying. He turned his back on her screaming form as she flew over the edge of the building. Thatcher heard Kerr cry out in anguish as he released the small hold he had kept on him.

Instantly, Thatcher felt the wrath fill every inch of his body. He shoved past Tahlia just in time to get to Hadley as Absalom brought his fist up to hit her. Thatcher lunged at him and grabbed him by the neck. He squeezed with all his might as he felt the life drain from his enemy's body.

"Thatcher no!" Tahlia screamed. "It's not Absalom. You're going to kill her!"

Thatcher didn't understand what she was saying at first, he felt his hands around Absalom's throat, he saw him in front of him; of course he was there. He was saving Hadley, he wasn't going to kill her.

"Finish it." Absalom choked out.

Thatcher squeezed harder and was surprised when he saw Absalom smile, wink and slowly fade away. His hands were wrapped around Hadley's neck. Her eyes were open, blood vessels had ruptured; she had tears running down her face.

"No." Thatcher cried as he slowly lowered Hadley to the ground. She was dead.

Chapter Twelve: Tahlia

Tahlia was staring at the dead body of her daughter as she was cradled in the arms of her killer. This was not going to happen.

She reached within her and felt her abilities restored. As long as Hadley was dead, she didn't share her power with anyone. Tahlia launched herself at Thatcher. When she hit him she knocked him backwards into the small wall near the edge of the building. He hit his head and stopped moving, he was unconscious.

Tahlia closed her eyes and focused on the cells in Hadley's body. She willed them to live. She willed her heart to beat. She forced the blood to move through her veins as she began compressions on her daughter's chest.

"C'mon Had. I know you can do this. I need you here. Whitley didn't die for this, she died so you could live."

Tahlia focused on Hadley's crushed windpipe. If she couldn't repair the windpipe it wouldn't matter if she got her heart beating again.

Precious seconds ticked by as she willed the broken pieces of her little girl to knit back together. She felt Nora kneel down next to her. Kerr took his post on the other side of Hadley's body. He leaned down and listened to her chest.

"She's alive. Her heart is beating. It's faint but it's there. If we can get her awake, I can heal her." Kerr told them.

For the first time since she'd been trying to get Hadley's body to cooperate, she noticed that her daughter's eyes had closed as though sleeping. She no longer had the terrifying death stare etched on her face.

Tahlia felt a surge of hope rush through her body. It was almost as though her true purpose had renewed within her. Now that Hadley was alive again, Tahlia couldn't use her abilities.

As difficult as it was for her, Tahlia had to focus on Thatcher. She went to him and examined his head. He would be awake soon and she had to figure out how to get him to see that there was still hope so he could safely release his anger.

Nora came up to her and helped her prop Thatcher up.

"We need to get Hadley and Thatcher back to the house." Nora told her gently.

Tahlia had a flash of a memory and remembered seeing Nora fly off the building. She reached over and pulled Nora into a fierce hug.

"Are you alright? What happened?" She questioned as she held her at arms-length and looked her over.

"I panicked at first. But as I fell I saw Kerr nearly fling himself over the edge after me and I knew I had to get back to him. Apparently my ability works when I'm falling from skyscrapers too." Nora told her with a shrug.

90

"I'm so glad you're alright. Everything happened so quickly I didn't have time to react. I wasn't able to stop Thatcher from hurting Hadley." Tahlia said sadly.

Nora glanced over at Kerr as he tried to wake Hadley. When she turned to face Tahlia again she had tears in her eyes. Tahlia knew that Nora and Hadley had become close over the last five years. Losing Whitley had drawn them closer together than simply being two of the Evolved could ever have done.

"She's waking!" Kerr exclaimed as he leaned over Hadley.

Tahlia came up to them and saw Hadley looking around in a panic. She was terrified and couldn't speak. Kerr put a hand on her head to calm her. She visibly relaxed as the green light wound around her neck and torso. Tahlia took Hadley's hand and gently kissed her forehead.

The light slowly dissipated until all that was left were faint bruises around her neck.

When she opened her eyes again, the blood vessels were almost healed.

"That's the most I can do. Her body was badly injured, she'll need a lot of rest, but she will be alright." Kerr told Tahlia and Nora, his exhaustion was evident

Hadley tried to sit up but grimaced slightly. Nora instructed her to lie down and wait until they were sure she was alright before she took her home. Hadley nodded her head slightly.

Nora went to Thatcher again and called Tahlia over.

"Tahlia, Kerr will stay with Hadley for now. I'm going to take you and Thatcher to Malcolm's grave. Romulus will join you. I think Thatcher needs to be reminded of the sacrifices people who love him have made. And seeing Romulus alive will show him that he isn't just like Absalom." Nora told her.

Tahlia nodded her head. This was a good plan. She needed to show him that despite his actions, he wasn't a lost cause. He needed to understand that this was not his nature to act this way.

Nora grabbed Thatcher and Tahlia and transported them to the clearing where Malcolm had been buried. She left them there to wait for Romulus.

Tahlia spoke gently to Thatcher, trying to wake him. He groaned and reached for his head. When he opened his eyes he saw Tahlia and began to sob.

"I killed them. I killed Romulus. I killed Nora. I killed Hadley. I'm so sorry." Thatcher choked out in anguish. "Please kill me. I don't deserve to live."

Tahlia shook her head and sat down next to Thatcher. She knew he was still dangerous, but she had to show him that she was willing to trust him.

"Hadley did die. But when she died, I was able to use her abilities to repair the damage that was done to her body. Kerr helped her to wake up and healed her more once she regained consciousness. She will be alright." Tahlia told him.

"But Romulus..." Thatcher began, but stopped short as he saw the large man break through the lilac bushes.

"I'm here son." Romulus told him. "I'm alive. You called for Nora when you left me in the alley. She got there in time to bring Kerr to help me."

Thatcher looked at him in shock. Tahlia could see that the tactics they were using were working. This was the longest she had seen him maintain his usual demeanor since she'd encountered him on the rooftop.

"And Nora?" Thatcher asked with hope breaking through his pained tone.

"How else do you think we got here?" Tahlia asked him. "She transported herself back to the roof as she fell."

Thatcher was crying in relief. He had hurt his family, but they were going to be alright. Tahlia touched his arm and he let her instead of reacting in anger.

"We brought you here to remind you that there are people who love you. You are still carrying a lot of grief and anger from losing Malcolm. But you have to understand that it was not your fault. Malcolm chose to sacrifice himself for you because he knew you were to play an important role in the future of the world. Malcolm gave his life for yours because he had hope that you and the other Evolved could stop Absalom." Tahlia told him.

Thatcher was crying, but he was listening. She could see the darkness in him beginning to leave.

"We're here because we love you. We all know you weren't trying to hurt any of us. It is evident that your anger manifested itself in the only way your brain would understand it. Absalom was the source of a lot of pain in your life, he was also the source of a lot of anger. Do you remember why you were able to defeat him?" Tahlia asked gently.

"Love." Thatcher replied between sobs.

"Yes. Your ability to love is what made it possible for you to overcome the most evil being the world has ever known. Do you understand what happened to you today?" Tahlia asked him.

"One of the Maladies. I knew when I saw him in the shadows, I can't explain how, but I knew. When he grabbed me, I couldn't stop the anger from building within me. It was Rage wasn't it?" Thatcher asked with more clarity than he had shown yet.

"Yes. You had skin to skin contact with one of the strongest and deadliest of the evils from the golden sphere. He touched you and you became infected. You continued to struggle against the evil infecting you because you are full of love and light." Tahlia said.

Thatcher took a deep breath and closed his eyes. Tahlia saw the darkness gather in his chest and disappear like smoke. He visibly relaxed, then fell into her lap weeping.

Chapter Thirteen: Hadley

Hadley lay on the roof staring up at the sky. She had only been awake for a few moments and everything was still a little blurry.

She remembered Thatcher coming at her with murder in his eyes, but he wasn't looking at her. She remembered him grabbing her and squeezing her throat. She remembered being desperate for air. Then she remembered white.

She was in the white expanse where she had said goodbye to Whitley. She knew this was death. Hadley had turned at the sound of a voice calling her name. It was Whitley.

"Had! What are you doing here?" Whitley demanded.

"Hi Whit." Hadley said quietly.

"What are you doing here?" Whitley demanded again.

"Well..." Hadley began.

"Hadley, what happened?" Whitley asked gently.

"I died." Hadley replied simply.

"You what?" Whitley asked breathlessly.

"I died. Thatcher, he went crazy. He killed me." Hadley told her sister.

Whitley looked at her with concern. Hadley was still confused about what had happened to her and even more confused about why it had happened. She was trying desperately to hold the pain of leaving her family at bay.

"You can't stay here." Whitley told her.

Hadley looked at her sister in surprise.

"Where am I supposed to go?" Hadley asked as her voice cracked. "I'm dead Whitley. My boyfriend got possessed and killed me. My best friend was thrown from a skyscraper. And now I can't even stay with you?"

Whitley's eyes widened in surprise. "That's not what I meant Hadley! I mean you're not going to die today."

"Whitley, I kind of already did." Hadley replied.

She watched in surprise as her sister took a step back and opened her arms.

"Was this part of the plan? Is this what was supposed to happen?" Whitley yelled.

"Whitley, what are you doing?" Hadley asked in shock.

"You'll see." Whitley told her.

"Come on! I need to know. Is this part of your plan?" Whitley yelled again.

Hadley felt a rush of wind whirl around them as figures appeared in the white expanse. She couldn't believe what she was seeing. There were other people surrounding them, they looked like Greek gods and goddesses. Their long flowing clothes were white and glowing.

"Hello Whitley." Said a pleasant woman with long silvery hair that fell in a straight line down her back.

"Lida!" Whitley said as she reached out to hug the woman.

"Hello Hadley." Lida said with a smile.

"Sorry, who are you?" Hadley asked.

"Oh! These are the other Old Immortals." Whitley said as though it was no big deal.

"You mean the dead ones?" Hadley asked bluntly.

A chorus of laughter surrounded her as the Old Immortals found humor in her statement. She looked around at each of them, unsure of what was really going on.

"We never truly died, we only faded away as our descendants were murdered." Said a short, portly man with a fair skin and white blond hair.

"You know Had, cloud of witnesses and all that?" Whitley said as she elbowed her sister.

"Alright, but what are you doing here?" Hadley asked.

"This is our home. We are here, just waiting for the time when we are needed again." The man replied.

"Okay. But why are you here now? I don't mean to be rude, but if I'm dead I'd rather just hang out with my sister." Hadley said in a snarky tone.

"Hadley, we're here because you need us." The man told her.

"Who are you?" Hadley asked.

"I am Marcellus." He smiled at her.

"Alright Marcellus, how can you help me?" Hadley asked.

"You're not supposed to die today." Said another one of the women. She had a kind face with wide set narrow eyes and short black hair.

"This is Charis." Whitley told Hadley.

"Okay Charis, if I'm not supposed to die, then what am I doing here?" Hadley asked.

"The Maladies." Replied Charis.

Hadley was beyond confused, she was starting to get frustrated. If she wasn't supposed to be dead she shouldn't be here. She shouldn't have been choked to death by the man she loved. If there was anything she had learned so far it was that no one could be brought back from the dead. She had been trying to find ways to resurrect Whitley and had found nothing but huge brick walls blocking her from any answers. Whether she was supposed to be or not, she was dead.

"I know what you're thinking Hadley. That this is impossible and we aren't going to be able to change anything. But, if we've learned anything through the years, it's that there are rules that can't be broken; but those rules can change at any moment." Said a man with white hair and chocolate colored skin.

Hadley stared at him dumbfounded.

"I'm Lucien by the way." He told her with a kind smile.

"Hadley, you can't stay here. You weren't supposed to die today and they're going to help send you back." Whitley told her.

"Even now your mother is using your abilities to knit the broken links in your body back together. You don't have much time left here if you want to say goodbye to your sister." The final Old Immortal told her gently. He looked as though he had been out in the sun his entire life; a golden tan and a dusting of blond highlights in his brown hair.

"That's Rance." Whitley whispered as she pulled her sister in for a hug.

"Whit, I'm tired of having to say goodbye to you. Every time I dream of you it hurts just as much as the day you left." Hadley told her sister as she squeezed her tightly.

"I know." Whitley replied just before she disappeared.

Hadley had opened her eyes on the rooftop feeling disoriented. She was looking up at a bright blue sky, laying on a hard cement roof. Kerr had told her to relax and wait for Nora to come back for them.

"Kerr, can we go yet? It's been a long day. I want to get home." Hadley said in a voice that was barely a whisper.

"Of course. Let me call Nora and see if we're safe to come home now." Kerr replied gently.

Soon, Nora appeared on the rooftop. She looked distraught, but appeared relieved to find Hadley breathing and awake. Hadley gave her a small smile when Nora came over and took her hand.

"Tahlia is helping Thatcher. We think he will be alright. Are you ready to go home?" Nora asked her.

Hadley nodded her head gingerly and soon found herself lying on the couch in the library.

Chapter Fourteen: Dorian

To say a lot had happened since he'd woken up that morning would have been the understatement of the century. Tahlia and Romulus had managed to talk Thatcher back from the edge, literally and figuratively. He was still beating himself up about what had happened. He still hadn't been able to talk to Hadley.

After Nora and Kerr returned they had whisked Keira off to open her presents, it hadn't been the birthday they had imagined for her. But little Keira took it all in stride, she had been very helpful through the entire day. Her birthday had been severely disrupted, but she spent the day helping her family without complaining once.

Dorian found himself sitting in the library with Romulus and Tahlia. They stared in different directions in silence. Hadley had shared her experience with them when she had returned home. The Virtues had been hit hard by the idea that their brothers and sisters were still there watching and waiting for a time when they would be needed. It showed them that the Creator had not forgotten them, it renewed their belief in what they had been called to do.

"So they've been here all along, just waiting." Tahlia said in awe.

"Now we know we have a reunion to look forward to when our time on Earth is done." Romulus replied.

Dorian nodded his head but continued to stare at the bookshelf in silence. He was pleased to know they were all still in existence, but he didn't know if it was better for him to know they were there somewhere, or for him to think they were gone forever. Dorian closed his eyes and sighed.

"What's troubling you brother?" Romulus asked with a hint of concern.

"I just don't know what we are expected to do next. Every minute of our lives since the day we were given the prophecies had been so focused on finding and protecting the Evolved. In the days since Thatcher defeated Absalom I have felt as though my life has no direction." Dorian told them.

"Don't think like that Dorian. Our lives have always been and will always be dedicated to the mission we were given by the Creator. If we are still here, our mission isn't over." Tahlia told him.

"That I know, I just wish we had more direction. I long for the days when the Creator would summon us." Dorian replied.

"Those days were meant to end. We know that through it all, we were meant to come to this moment. If Pandora had not released the Maladies, we would not have Tahlia in our lives. We wouldn't have left Greece when we did, which would mean we wouldn't have moved to Central America. If we hadn't moved to Central America, we wouldn't have mated with human women, and we wouldn't have any descendants to defeat Absalom." Romulus told him firmly.

Dorian knew he was right. Without all of those events they could be living in a very different world; if Absalom hadn't killed them all. After the Maladies were released, the Old Immortals had decided to take their leave of Greece. Absalom had not been allowed to accompany them; he had been banished to hell when the Creator learned of his involvement in the Pandora situation. At the time, they were unaware of Silas' involvement in his plans. The Council moved to Central America because it was largely unpopulated; after the way things went with Pandora, they knew their influence had grown too strong for humans to handle.

"One thing is certain, we may not know what to expect next, but we promised the Creator we would stay the course." Tahlia told them both.

Dorian and Romulus nodded in agreement. They would never break a promise they had made to the Creator. Dorian tried to shake the feelings of uncertainty he had been

GROWING hope

experiencing and focus instead on what had happened with Rage.

"They're getting braver." Dorian said more to himself than the others.

"They are, but the braver they get the more likely it is that we'll catch them and destroy them." Romulus replied.

"They can sense that I'm getting weaker. I've been waiting to tell you both, but I have no power of my own left. I put the rest of my ability into Hadley when I brought her back. I believe I am mortal." Tahlia told them steadily.

"You're not mortal yet. You are still the hope of the Present Era." Dorian told her. "You no longer have the abilities gifted to you as an Old Immortal, but you cannot lose the spirit that created you in the first place until the new hope takes your place."

Tahlia looked surprised. Dorian knew she hadn't been aware of the extent to which he had researched her origin story. Through his research he discovered that in each era, the spirit of hope would chose a vessel to act as the hope of mankind for that era. Tahlia was the vessel that had been created for the present era, she was the first and only vessel hope had chosen. But, as the Present Era came to an end a new vessel would be chosen and Tahlia would be completely mortal.

"I think there are pieces missing from the puzzle that makes up our history." Dorian told her.

Romulus and Tahlia nodded in agreement.

"I've found little about where you came from, but I don't believe you were one of the Old Immortals from the beginning. I believe you were brought to us later." Dorian said.

"I don't remember anything." Tahlia replied. "I only remember being with you all, and that you all treated me like a little sister."

"Well, I believe you are truly our little sister. From what I've read and the conversations I've had with Romulus, we've discerned that neither of us can remember much from before you arrived, and the details of your arrival are absent altogether." Dorian told her. "But, I think it's time I share what I've learned and what I've guessed based on what few memories I do have."

Tahlia leaned forward and listened as Romulus and Dorian shared their knowledge and memories regarding her purpose and future.

Chapter Fifteen: Nora

It had been nearly a month since their experiences on the rooftop in Chicago. Thatcher, Kerr and Romulus had gotten wind of the whereabouts of Chaos. She was one of the Maladies that usually flew under the radar, but her meddlesome activities had recently caused a lot of trouble in Las Vegas.

She wasn't one of the evils that directly injured humans and didn't generally infect them with her brand of crazy. But, she was having a blast making everyone a winner in Sin City. Every casino was in upheaval as they tried to determine how they would stay in business if they had to pay every gambler in the place.

Nora knew they would have to destroy her when they caught her, but this was one Malady she didn't fear. If she was being honest, she actually thought Chaos had a certain flair that she found quite amusing.

"Mommy!"

Nora heard Keira yelling for her from the back yard where she had been playing all morning. Something about her tone caused Nora to rush to her daughter's side. She didn't think Keira was hurt or scared, but something was different.

She found Keira standing in the middle of the yard. She was alone, but appeared to be looking at something with great interest.

"What is it baby?" Nora asked as she knelt down next to her child, trying to get the same perspective Keira had.

"Mom! I saw Hadley out here but she couldn't hear me. She came from there." Keira said pointing to the tall reeds on the edge of the pond at the edge of the property.

"What would Hadley be doing there? Are you sure you saw her?" Nora asked her with interest.

Keira rolled her eyes in exasperation, it was such a grown up response that Nora had to keep herself from laughing at the little girl.

"Yes mommy. She came out of the tall grass and looked around like she was lost, then she went back in the grass like she didn't know she was even out." Keira told her with concern in her voice.

Nora was a little troubled by this information, she didn't know what Hadley would be doing out there. Hadley hadn't left her room much since her experience in Chicago.

"What are we looking at?" Hadley asked behind her.

Nora nearly jumped out of her skin and Keira yelped in surprise.

"How did you get over here so fast?" Keira asked as she launched herself at Hadley for a hug.

"I came down to the kitchen to get something to drink and saw you two out here staring off into the distance. I thought maybe you needed my help." Hadley replied with caution in response to the looks she was getting from Nora and Keira.

"But you were over there, and you looked lost. Hey! You changed your clothes too." Keira said in a small accusatory voice.

Hadley looked at Nora and shrugged her shoulders. "I haven't been outside at all today. And this is what I put on after I showered this morning. No wardrobe changes for me today."

Nora looked at Keira with concern. They began walking towards the reeds.

"There you are again!" Keira cried out pointing at the same spot she had claimed Hadley was moments ago.

Nora and Hadley looked at each other in surprise. Hadley was walking right along beside them. Keira was still seeing her in the distance. There was only one person who could be mistaken for Hadley, and they both knew it.

"Keira, can you take me to the other Hadley?" Nora asked her little girl.

Keira nodded firmly and took her mother's hand. The three of them began running towards the reeds near the pond. It was a beautiful day in late August. The heat wasn't as intense at it had been only a few short weeks ago. The South Dakota fall was quickly approaching, but they still had a few more weeks of fair weather before everything began to prepare for the winter months.

When they arrived at the reeds, Hadley pulled them apart and poked her head inside.

Hadley pulled back and gave Nora a look that clearly told her there was nothing there. Perhaps Keira's abilities were layering the past with the present.

"There's no one here honey. Are you sure this is where you saw the other Hadley?" Nora asked carefully.

"Of course it is." Keira furrowed her eyebrows and gave both her mother and Hadley a look that told them she was confused and frustrated.

Keira was the type of girl that had to look for herself. She took a step forward and looked in to the reeds. She let out an exasperated sigh and looked back at Nora and Hadley. Nora smiled at her little girl as she looked back in to the reeds and took a step forward trying to get a better look. She was nothing if not thorough.

"I don't get it." Keira said. "She was here. She was right in there."

Keira pointed to the pond. A moment later she screamed in shock and surprise, disappearing into the reeds. Nora leapt through in search of her daughter, but she was nowhere to be seen.

Hadley and Nora began frantically calling out to Keira but were greeted with silence. Her daughter was gone.

Chapter Sixteen: Keira

"Mommy?" Keira asked tentatively as she poked her head back out through the tall grass.

Her mom and Hadley were gone. She was all alone. She looked around and saw that the pond looked the same as it always had, but it didn't seem as bright. It was almost like when her mom made a copy of a picture and the colors weren't quite the same. It was dull and quiet. There were no bug sounds, the wind didn't blow, no birds calling to each other. Instinctively, she knew she was only in a copy of the world she lived in.

"Hello? Other Hadley?" Keira called out.

"Who are you?"

Keira turned around to see a girl who looked just like Hadley standing by the edge of the pond. Her long blond hair was flowing freely around her upper arms. She wore a pretty white sundress and no shoes.

"My name is Keira. Are you Hadley?" She asked the girl.

"You know Hadley?" The girl asked Keira.

"She's my aunt, kind of." Keira told the girl. "But you look just like her."

"I'm Whitley." Whitley replied.

"No. You're wrong. Whitley is dead. Everyone still misses her." Keira said sadly.

"I'm not dead. I'm lost. I can't find the house. I'm sure they think I died, but I didn't. I jumped at Hadley, then woke up here." Whitley replied.

Keira shook her head. "Are you crazy?"

Whitley laughed and knelt down so she was face to face with Keira. A look of recognition crossed her face as she looked at Keira.

"Oh my gosh. Are you Nora's baby?" She asked in disbelief.

Keira had been studying Whitley, unsure of what to make of her and the situation she found herself in. Hadley told her about her twin many times, always with sorrow in her voice. Keira knew she was gone and that there was no way to bring her back. Hadley had been trying.

"Yes." Keira responded to her question.

"But, how can that be? How are you so big? Just yesterday you were in your mommy's tummy, she was barely pregnant." Whitley was desperately trying to rationalize the existence of the little girl in front of her.

"That wasn't yesterday. Whitley, you've been gone for almost 5 years." Keira told her gently.

"No. That can't be right. I was only with them this morning." Whitley looked shocked and afraid.

Keira didn't know how, but she knew she needed to help her. She knew Whitley wasn't a ghost; ghosts weren't real. But memories sometimes left an impression on the world. Maybe Whitley was a memory.

"You said you're lost?" Keira asked.

Whitley nodded her head and bit her lip. If Keira could help her find her way, maybe she wouldn't be lost anymore and she could go to heaven.

"Let me help you find your way." Keira told her.

Whitley took Keira's hand and stood up, trying her best to look brave, but Keira could see the fear and uncertainty etched in her face.

"You need help finding the house right?" Keira asked her.

"Yes. I remember this pond, and these reeds, but every time I think I've found the way out, the house isn't there." Whitley replied.

"Let me take you there." Keira told her.

Keira held Whitley's hand and led her through the tall grass. It was strange to come out on the other side and see the lawn and house look so empty. As they walked toward the house, Whitley gripped Keira's hand tightly. She smiled a little when

Whitley gasped as the house came into view.

"You found it!" Whitley exclaimed as she began to press forward, keeping a firm grip on Keira's hand.

As they neared the back door of the house, everything started to get brighter. Keira watched with curiosity as the copy of our world seemed to snap back into place. When she opened the back door, she felt a slight resistance and realized Whitley seemed to be struggling to cross the threshold. Keira furrowed her brow, and gave her a firm tug. Whitley came through with a 'pop' that only Keira seemed to hear.

Her mom and Hadley were standing in the breakfast nook with Dorian. They looked up in surprise as Keira seemed to materialize in front of them. It was only then that they registered who had come with her.

"Whitley?" Hadley asked in awe.

Keira hadn't helped Whitley move on, she had brought her back.

Chapter Seventeen: Whitley

She stood in the kitchen with her sister and Nora. Dorian had rushed off to call the others. Hadley had nearly collapsed in her arms after taking a few tentative steps toward her.

"Has it really been five years?" Whitley asked.

"Yes. You saved Hadley's life at the cost of your own." Nora told her.

"So does that mean I'm your little sister now?" Whitley asked.

She didn't know if she had aged while she was in Hadley's mind, she couldn't even remember being there. Every time she tried to remember, she would start to feel nauseated. Hadley and Nora had taken turns filling her in on everything that had happened since the day they fought Absalom. She was still struggling to wrap her mind around it all when Nora abruptly told them she would be back, and disappeared.

"She went to get everyone else. They were in Las Vegas dealing with Chaos." Hadley told her.

Whitley didn't know what to say. So much had changed since she'd been gone. Whitley smiled at her sister. She had so many emotions whirling around inside her. She was so happy to be back and to be part of their lives again, but she was so overwhelmed by all the things that had happened since she'd been gone. The idea that the evil beings that had been contained within the sphere were out and walking around in human form was a lot to take in. Their mother was in danger, Keira was a four year old powerhouse and Thatcher had lost his marbles.

"Do you think me coming back had to do with you dying? It can't be a coincidence that this all happened so close together." Whitley told her.

"I don't know. But, I do remember one of the Old Immortals telling me that the rules that can't be broken are always changing. I wasn't supposed to die that day, so I came back. Maybe you weren't supposed to die either?" Hadley said with uncertainty.

"Then why have I been gone so long?" Whitley asked.

Hadley didn't seem to have any answers for that, she just reached over and took her sisters hand. Whitley didn't want to become a concern for her family. She was alive, she was here, she just wanted to live and be here and not worry about the 'why' and 'how'.

"So, Thatcher went nuts and killed you. How's that impacted your relationship?" Whitley asked her with only a hint of sarcasm.

"Well, I forgave him the moment I woke up. I knew he thought he was seeing Absalom. He didn't know he was hurting me. The problem is, he hasn't forgiven himself." Hadley told her.

"I'm sorry Had." Whitley could practically feel the pain radiating from her sister.

"Me too. You have no idea." Hadley replied sadly. "But, I'm glad you're here. I've missed this. I've missed you!" Hadley pulled her sister into a tight hug. "I never gave up hope that we could bring you back."

Whitley didn't respond, she just held her sister as they both shed a few tears. She knew she wasn't going through the same emotional reunion her sister was experiencing. No time had passed for her, but Hadley had endured five years without her sister.

Nora must have brought everyone back with her in a different room because Whitley could hear voices coming from the foyer. One of them was her mother. She looked up, releasing Hadley in time to be attacked by Tahlia.

Her mother held her close, touched her face, hair, and arms, then held her hands.

She had never seen her mother so happy, it was a lovely sight.

"I don't understand it, but I'll take it." Tahlia told her.

Kerr and Romulus were discussing something and gesturing towards Whitley. They seemed troubled by something but didn't appear to be ready to share it. Whitley was starting to get tired and longed to lie down in her bed. A thought hit her that hadn't occurred to her before.

"Do I still have a room?" She asked.

Everyone laughed in response and assured her that she did still have a room. Hadley had insisted on keeping everything as it had been in case she found a way to bring her sister back. Whitley loved being with all of them, but she wanted desperately to be alone to process everything she'd been told. She didn't want to leave the house for fear she wouldn't find her way back.

She had been thinking a lot about how she had managed to find the house. Before

Keira showed up she had been getting frustrated. She didn't know how the little girl had done it, but she firmly believed that Keira was the reason she was standing with her family now.

Whitley looked over at Keira. The little girl had been silent since she had reunited Whitley with the family. It was clear that she was just as confused about her involvement in bringing her back as Whitley was herself. No one had brought up the logistics of her return, but she knew it was something they needed to discuss.

"Let's go sit down." Whitley said, gesturing towards the library.

Everyone filed down the hallway, talking excitedly amongst themselves. Whitley noticed that Thatcher hung back, looking nervous about joining everyone. Whitley had hardly been back an hour and she was already tired of the mopey Thatcher.

"Hey you." Whitley said poking him in the arm.

"What?" Thatcher asked her defensively.

"Knock it off. Seriously. I haven't been here to deal with it, but Hadley and Nora filled me in. She knows it wasn't you. So quit being so stupid." Whitley told him.

Thatcher looked at her for a moment, clearly surprised by her words. He started to say something but Whitley decided she wasn't finished.

"You killed her. You killed her because you thought you had to kill Absalom all over again. Guess what? The bad guys were screwing with you. You need to be Thatcher again and stop acting like you have to pay for what happened." Whitley said with finality.

Thatcher pulled her into a quick hug then drew back to look at her. "I've missed you."

Whitley laughed and punched him in the arm. He had become a brother to her and she hated seeing the tortured look on his face.

"But seriously, you need to talk to Hadley. You guys love each other and if you keep wandering around like this you're going to lose her." Whitley told him before walking past him to enter the library.

Whitley took a seat in between Hadley and Tahlia, allowing each of them to take her hand. Dorian was pacing the library while everyone watched him, waiting for him to say what was on his mind. To her surprise, Kerr was the first to break the silence.

"Whitley, we have something to tell you." Kerr said gesturing to Romulus. "From the moment we saw you, we knew something had changed."

"Spit it out Kerr." Whitley told him impatiently.

"Neither of us can sense any power coming from you." Romulus told her.

"Okay." Whitley replied in confusion.

"You don't have any abilities. You're still Hadley's twin, you're still a descendant of

Tahlia, but you're no longer one of the Evolved." Kerr told her gently.

"But can I still be in your club?" Whitley asked in her best valley girl accent.

Everyone laughed loudly at her response. Kerr and Romulus seemed relieved that she wasn't upset or concerned. Quite honestly, Whitley didn't care if she had power or not. When she had it before, it didn't feel like it was hers. She didn't understand it at the time because it was all so new.

"I don't need abilities. I think all that power was supposed to be Hadley's anyway. As long as I don't have to leave I couldn't care less." Whitley told them.

"I think we have a few things we need to discuss. Thatcher, can you please take Keira out to play?" Dorian asked.

Thatcher nodded and reached for Keira's hand. The little girl smiled widely and took his hand allowing him to lead her from the room. Once they had left, Nora and Kerr took a seat on the couch opposite the one

Whitley, Hadley and Tahlia were occupying. Dorian sat in one of the oversized armchairs and began stroking his beard.

"Keira brought me back." Whitley said aloud. "It was the strangest thing. I couldn't find my way out of the reeds. I was frustrated, I was scared. I finally gave up and sat down on the edge of the pond. I didn't understand why I couldn't get out, it felt hopeless."

Her family seemed enraptured by her explanation, so she continued.

"As soon as I decided I wasn't going to find my way out, I heard a little girl. When I turned around, I saw Keira standing there. She had appeared out of nowhere. Her presence was so soothing, it made me feel like if anyone could help me, she could." Whitley told them. "As we walked across the lawn, it was like the house appeared out of the mist. But, when I tried to come into the house, it felt like trying to walk through Jello. Keira pulled me through and suddenly everything seemed to right itself."

Dorian leaned forward, resting his arms on his thighs. He looked at Whitley for a moment more before glancing at Kerr and Nora. His eyes finally landed on Tahlia.

"It is as I thought. As the Evolved come closer to ending the Present Era, the spirit of hope must find a new vessel." He told them.

Dorian went on to explain the theories he had shared with Tahlia about how she came to be and how the new hope would be chosen.

"I firmly believe that Keira is the new vessel. She has found a way to intervene in a number of situations that all shared the same theme; hopelessness. In all of those situations, she has been able to provide hope and renew the fire within someone in their moment of need." Dorian told them calmly.

Nora and Kerr exchanged a look. Whitley felt Tahlia squeeze her hand, almost imperceptibly. She squeezed back, knowing that her mother was probably afraid of what that life could mean for Keira.

Chapter Eighteen: Kerr

Kerr tucked his daughter in and kissed her dark curly head. She sighed in her sleep and he sat to watch her for a few more moments. From their conversation in the library he had learned that this sweet little girl was going to play an important role in the New Era.

Dorian's research had only gotten him so far because there wasn't a lot of information available about the spirit of hope. Because Tahlia had been the only vessel, little was known about how or when Keira would assume the role. Tahlia had sprung from the sphere as a fully grown woman with no memory of a life before her arrival. Did she have a life before she became the vessel? Had she once been someone's little girl with hopes and dreams of her own? Did she exist in physical form at all prior to being released from the sphere?

There were so many questions but so few answers. None of them were certain what would happen in Keira's life and that terrified Kerr more than anything. He stood carefully so as not to disturb his daughters sleep.

He made his way to the bedroom he shared with Nora and found her curled up on their king sized bed waiting for him. Her green eyes met his as he walked in the room.

"She's asleep." Kerr told her softly.

"I'm worried about her." Nora told him as tears sprang to her eyes.

"So am I." Kerr replied as he joined her on the bed and pulled her close.

Nora rolled over so she was face to face with her husband. She leaned up to kiss his jaw and snaked an arm around his waist. Kerr loved moments like this with his wife. Aside from Keira, Nora was his entire world; he had wholly and completely given himself to her, heart and soul.

"She will be alright. She has a strong support system. We're all going to help her in any way we can." Kerr tried to reassure her.

"You're darn right we will!" Nora said as she gave him a gentle shove.

Kerr laughed at his wife and adjusted his body so he could kiss her, Nora returned his kiss fervently. They took advantage of the private moment to ignite the passion between them.

As they dressed for bed, Kerr admired Nora's perfect body. No words could express how much he loved that woman, he felt so much pride in the idea that she had chosen him. Nora caught his eye and threw a pillow at him as he took in the sight of her.

"What are you looking at?" Nora said as she pulled her tank top over her head.

"The perfection that is you." Kerr told her, plopping back on the bed.

"Right. I'm so perfect. Slightly lumpy, stretch marks, and boobs that are starting to sag." She laughed.

"You know exactly what I mean. Perfection doesn't mean flawless. Your body has given us an amazing gift. Your body has given me so many pleasurable moments...." Kerr wiggled his eyebrows in a seductive manner.

"Oh dear Lord." Nora snorted as she lay down next to him.

"You don't have to call me that right now." Kerr told her.

"Blasphemer!" Nora feigned shock before giggling at her husband.

Kerr pulled her into his arms and adjusted his body so he was wrapped around hers in an arc. He felt Nora relax as he held her, indicating that she had fallen asleep. Kerr closed his eyes and tried to fall asleep as well but found himself to be restless. He gently released Nora and rolled over.

He sat up on the edge of the bed and looked around the room. The chaise by the window was bathed in moonlight, he crossed the room to pull the curtains closed. When he looked out the window, he saw Whitley sitting in the grass in the middle of the large back yard. Kerr wasn't sure what she was doing, but he decided to go check it out.

He made his way downstairs as quietly as possible and eased the back door open. Kerr carefully approached Whitley, afraid he would startle her if she hadn't heard him coming.

"Hi Kerr." Whitley said.

"Hey Whitley, what are you doing out here?" Kerr asked her.

"Meditating." She replied without looking at him.

"Can I join you?" Kerr asked, sitting down without waiting for an answer.

They sat for a few moments in silence, staring out into the rapidly darkening night. Kerr wondered how Whitley had adjusted so quickly to the discovery that she had been gone for nearly five years. She had told them it was like she closed her eyes in one place and opened them in another; but Kerr was beginning to suspect she had begun to remember the rest of her time away.

"Whitley, I need you to answer something for me. Don't be upset, but I'm starting to sense something about you and I need you to be honest with me." Kerr told her quietly.

Whitley turned to face him in the grass and waited for him to continue.

"You're beginning to remember your time in the white expanse aren't you?" Kerr asked her.

"Yes." Whitley told him. "I remember it all now. That's why I was out here. I've been talking to the other Old Immortals. I can't see them, but I can hear them and they can hear me."

"Why did you lie and say you couldn't remember anything?" Kerr asked.

"I didn't at first. When I fell asleep, it all came back to me in a dream. Only, it wasn't a dream really. I saw the rest of the council and they told me that while I do not have abilities, I am going to be their bridge to the Evolved and the Virtues. They said we're going to need their help." Whitley replied.

"What do we need their help with?" Kerr asked her curiously.

"Here, let's try this." Whitley said holding her hands out to him with the palms up. "It will be easier for you to see."

Kerr reached out and placed his palms on hers.

A flash of white light sent him reeling as he found himself in a large white room. There were columns running along the edges and a wide set of stairs leading down on one end. It took him a moment to register Whitley standing next to him.

"Where are we?" Kerr asked.

Whitley shrugged her shoulders and looked around as though she expected to find something familiar. Voices were coming from the direction of the stairs, Kerr walked over to the top and looked down, vaguely aware of Whitley standing next to him again.

"Where did you find them?" A man asked someone in front of him.

"I was looking for a place to start a new city. You asked us to help you grow your world." Another man replied.

Shivers ran up and down Kerr's spine; he would recognize that voice anywhere. The first man shifted his weight, opening the line of sight to the other man; Absalom. Kerr felt Whitley grab his arm and tried to pull him back. Kerr stayed where he was, waiting for the conversation to continue.

"Bring them to me Absalom, you say they are repentant of their actions but I must see for myself." The first man told Absalom.

"Yes my Lord." Absalom replied with a deep bow.

Kerr watched the first man make his way up the stairs, catching a glimpse of his face as he drew closer. The Creator. But who was he asking Absalom about?

Everything began to wobble and shimmer as they appeared to stand still while the world moved in fast forward around them. Whitley had taken his hand in hers, he knew she was not accustomed to memory travel as he was. He squeezed her clammy hand in reassurance. Their surroundings slowed to a normal speed and they stood looking at the long table, now full of friendly faces.

The Creator stood at the head of the table waiting for something as he expectantly stared at the stairs. Kerr turned to see Absalom coming up the stairs with a band of beings behind him. At first glance, Kerr would have thought them to be human. There were eight in all, a few looked like someone you may meet on the street, but there were others who looked cold and dead. The least appealing was the appearance of the two who seemed to be suffering from a severe infection or injury. Whitley grabbed his shirt to get his attention, when Kerr turned to look at her, she mouthed one word. Maladies.

"Absalom, please introduce your guests." The Creator instructed as the Council of Immortals watched the newcomers warily.

"These are the beings I found while scouring the world for more places to grow civilizations. I have now been informed they are our predecessors." Absalom brazenly told the council.

"Is this true Father?" Dorian asked the Creator.

"Yes." The Creator replied sadly.

"How did they come to their present state?" Asked a man with deep brown skin.

"That's Lucien." Whitley whispered.

"Please, take a seat and I will tell you all a story." The Creator gestured for the Maladies to make themselves comfortable.

"As you know, when our world first began, it was empty. There was no one here, no animals or vegetation. It is true that I created the world in only seven days, but we all know time had different meaning then. I created light to fill the darkness, I created earth to stand on, I created the sky to hold the light. But before I went any further, I created angels. My angels were supposed to be my companions, my messengers, and my family. Some of those angels have lived up to those expectations, but some have fallen from grace." The Creator said as he glanced at the Maladies.

Kerr and Whitley exchanged confused looks.

"After I created you all to be the ambassadors to my next creation, man, I discovered that some of my angels were beginning to plot against me to destroy you. They were unhappy with my plans for you. They wanted to be the ones to have an impact on man. After I breathed life into the first men, the beings you see around you began to attempt to sway them towards their own selfish desires. When I uncovered their actions, I banished them from their place above with me. I sent them as far I could from myself and the creations I had brought to life." The Creator shook his head sadly.

"But where could you possibly send them?" A woman with black hair and narrow eyes asked him quietly.

"I created a place for them, deep within the Earth. I created the Underworld and banished them there, then I sealed the entrance. Their energies are so strong that they are still sometimes able to infect man, but they are not able to directly impact their lives. They can only take up residence in man's heart if he invites them in. If he does, then upon his death, his soul will be absorbed by the being whose sin he has portrayed." The Creator paused to see if there were more questions.

Kerr and Whitley stood watching the Maladies as they watched the Creator with great interest; their faces full of something that could almost be obsession. No one said anything as they processed the information the Creator had laid out in front of them.

"Absalom tells me you are repentant. Would any of you care to elaborate?" The Creator asked.

A young woman with wide, almost black eyes stood. She nodded her acknowledgement to the Council of Immortals, then settled her gaze on the Creator.

"Oh you are mistaken. We are not repentant. We simply wanted an audience with you. Had to see what all the fuss was about you know." She crossed her arms indignantly. "Not impressed."

"Chaos, you have tried to incite others against me by spreading your lies about who I am. You've led men to idol worship and sacrifice. Of course you are the one to stand against me now." The Creator said, his voice thick with hurt and grief.

Kerr watched as the Old Immortals prepared for a fight. But the Creator held his hand up to calm them. He glanced at Absalom who nodded his head and pulled something from his robe.

"The sphere!" Kerr exclaimed. He stepped closer to examine it, it had a golden hue but none of the glow it had in his visions.

"From this moment on, you will be held within this container. You will not see the light of day *again. You have proven to me that you are not to be trusted and you cannot be allowed to destroy the world we have worked so hard to create." The Creators voice thundered and shook the room. "I command your energies into the sphere. I command you, the maladies that have tainted my creations, to leave this place at once." With a wave of his hand, the Maladies were pulled into the sphere.*

Kerr and Whitley watched as their bodies appeared to morph and stretch and pull as they were sucked into the device meant to contain them for eternity. When their moans of despair had fallen silent, the room began to speed around them again. They watched the council come and go, nights and days passed until time finally seemed to snap back into place around them.

The Creator sat in meditation on the table in the otherwise empty room.

"We fear Absalom may have allowed the Maladies to have a greater impact on his consciousness than he has let on to you." A voice said from the shadows.

"I believe you are right." The Creator said calmly.

Two men stepped from the shadows near the stairs and approached the Creator. One was short with blond hair, the other was tall and tan.

"The short one is Marcellus. The Greek god is Rance." Whitley whispered.

"If we are to create woman, we must do something to keep the scales tipped in our favor." Rance told him.

"I agree. Bring me the sphere." The Creator said, still meditating.

Rance crossed the room and placed his palm against the smooth marble wall at the back of the large room. The wall shook and the marble slid aside to reveal the sphere resting on a blue velvet platform. Marcellus carefully lifted the sphere and brought it to the Creator.

"If Absalom accomplishes what I think he will, we need to have a failsafe way to ensure that the Maladies will not be able to do as they please. We must be able to offer man an alternative to the evils held within this sphere." The Creator told them as he took the sphere from Marcellus.

Kerr and Whitley watched in awe as the sphere began to vibrate and levitate. The Creator was concentrating on it with a furrowed brow. He seemed lost in thought.

"I must put a piece of myself in the sphere with them." The Creator told the two council members.

Both Rance and Marcellus seemed to regard the Creator stoically. They seemed to know better than to question how he came to this conclusion; they had full trust in their Creator.

The Creator reached up as though he were pulling a hair from his robe. Instead, he pulled a glowing mist from within him. The glowing mist swirled before him, hovering in midair. He held up his hands indicating that the mist should envelope the sphere. As the mist encircled the golden sphere, it slowly fused with it, giving it the ethereal glow Kerr had become accustomed to from his visions.

"What was that?" Marcellus asked in awe.

"The spirit of hope." The Creator said simply. "If the day comes that the sphere is broken and the Maladies are released into the world, the spirit of hope will manifest in a vessel. As long as the vessel lives, the Maladies cannot win."

The world around them shook and twisted as it disintegrated.

Kerr and Whitley locked eyes sitting on the lawn behind the house. Kerr was having trouble wrapping his head around what they'd just witnessed. They now knew the Creator had suspected Absalom's treachery and had prepared for it without his knowledge. They now knew why the Maladies wanted Tahlia dead. If she died, they would be able to do whatever they wanted, they would win. If or when Keira became the new vessel, she would always be a target. They would try to kill her.

Chapter Nineteen: Dorian

"What do you mean you were there?" Dorian asked.

"The rest of the council has been talking to me. They said we're going to need their help. Rance and Marcellus were part of the Creators plan against Absalom. If they hadn't contacted me, none of us would have known." Whitley told him indignantly.

"Alright. I just didn't think it was possible that there had been secrets between my brothers and me." Dorian told her.

"They didn't think Absalom would ever turn. At the time, the Creator didn't know who he could trust, but Rance and Marcellus had already sniffed out trouble. They had suspicions about Absalom when he showed up talking about happening upon these beings. The Creator knew there was no way he could 'happen' upon them." Whitley told him.

"That makes sense." Romulus replied.

"I wish I understood what had gotten into Absalom." Dorian said with a frustrated sigh.

"The council has a theory. When Absalom removed the seal from the Underworld, he was hit with an overwhelming amount of the pent up energies the Maladies had been hurling at their prison walls for so many years." Whitley replied.

"But he must have been open to the evils if they were able to infect him so easily." Kerr said suddenly.

Dorian agreed with Kerr. Something must have changed him before he found the Maladies. Absalom had always been so strong, so faithful; he had made mistakes, but it had been a shock to them all when he had convinced Pandora to open the sphere. That day they had lost Absalom, but they gained Tahlia.

"The part that has me the most amazed is that Tahlia is imbued with a piece of the Creator. No wonder she developed abilities to match our own. What we still don't know is where Tahlia came from and why she was chosen to be the vessel." Dorian told them all.

When Kerr and Whitley had finished with their late night travel through the memories of the other Old Immortals, they had fallen asleep in the library. They were exhausted from their efforts but wanted to be sure to speak with Dorian right away in the morning. When Dorian walked in he found them sleeping on the two couches with piles of books on either side of them. He assumed they had been trying to do some research into what they had learned. Dorian had awoken them, and immediately called out to Romulus with his mind after hearing the gist of what they'd seen.

"We have to tell my mom what we found out about her. We have to tell Nora about Keira's future." Whitley told them all sternly.

"Yes, I think we need to call a family meeting right away this morning." Dorian acquiesced.

Once they had gathered everyone in the library, Dorian nodded to Kerr and Whitley. They were the two who had experienced the memory, it was only right that they be the two who shared it.

Dorian watched his family for reactions as they absorbed the new information. His main concern was for the reaction of Tahlia and Nora. Keira was perched on her mother's lap listening intently. Thatcher and Hadley were actually sitting next to each other for the first time in weeks.

"So if the Creator didn't put me in the sphere as I am, who was I before?" Tahlia asked quietly as she looked at Keira.

"We don't know. I don't know if we ever will." Romulus told her softly.

"Is Keira going to forget everything if she becomes the next vessel?" Nora asked.

Dorian had anticipated this question but still didn't have any answers. They didn't know what would happen when that day came and their days of talking to the

Creator face to face were long gone. Kerr crossed to Nora and placed a comforting hand on her shoulder.

"I can't believe they were fallen angels." Hadley said softly.

"I had forgotten all about our encounter with them until Kerr and Whitley told us what they saw. Almost as though the memory had been there but had been just out of my grasp." Dorian told them honestly.

"Do you think the Creator would have blocked our memories?" Romulus asked his brother, voicing the question that had been in the back of Dorian's mind.

Dorian wasn't sure what reason there would be to block a memory such as that, but the Creator never did anything without reason. There must have been a purpose behind him preventing them from accessing those memories.

"If he did, he had good reason to." Dorian told his brother.

"They're talking again." Whitley told them.

Dorian watched curiously as Whitley tipped her head like a dog hearing a high-pitched sound. He wondered briefly what it would be like to hear their voices again. It had been centuries since he had seen and spoken with some of them, even longer for others. They had anticipated the loss of the men as their descendants were picked off one by one. But the surprisingly painful moments had come as they lost each of the women; they had no descendants, they had not been targeted by Absalom. They had waited for Tahlia to disappear but she never did. At the time, they had assumed that they were all still there because they were the Virtues, but they have since learned there was so much more to her story.

"They were called back by the Creator." Whitley said when she opened her eyes, staring directly at Dorian.

"Who?" He asked, suddenly confused.

"Charis and Lida. The Creator brought them home so their abilities could be saved. Now the rest of the council has become a collective. They can share their power amongst themselves. They are there to watch out for you and help the Evolved in the coming battles with the Maladies." Whitley told him.

"You know, cloud of witnesses and all that?" Hadley said smiling at Whitley.

Dorian processed this information as the twins shared an inside joke. It amazed him how many layers there were to the Creators plan. He had always had faith in the Creator and his vision for the future of the world. Dorian would never cease to be amazed by the moments when the pieces fell into place.

Chapter Twenty: Thatcher

The sudden reappearance of Whitley had left Thatcher reeling. It couldn't be a coincidence that she returned soon after he had killed her sister. He shook his head. He couldn't think of it like that, Hadley had told him numerous times that she didn't look at it that way and didn't hold any anger towards him.

He was happy for Hadley upon the return of her sister, he just didn't understand it. He had grown accustomed to not being able to comprehend the things that happened in his world, but he never would have dreamed that someone they lost would return. He glanced at Whitley to see her listening to the voices in her head again.

"So you're like a two way radio to the rest of the Old Immortals?" Thatcher asked Whitley.

"Something like that." Whitley replied with a grin. "Now shhhh."

It must have been strange to suddenly realize she could communicate with people in a completely different plane of existence. He wondered if they could hear her thoughts all the time or if they only tuned in when she had something to say to them.

He didn't want to think about someone being inside his mind all the time. Thatcher had been struggling with his own inner demons since the day he had been infected by Rage. He was still working through all the anger that surfaced that day. It got better every day, but he still feared that the anger would burn up in him again and make him lash out.

Despite the guilt he felt over what happened with Hadley, he reached over and took her hand. He felt a flood of relief when she gave it a small squeeze in response. Small gestures like this gave him more hope that they would indeed be able to move past that day on the roof. Hadley had tried to reassure him many times but part of him still held on to the fear and doubt that led him to believe she would never look at him the same way.

He realized with a start that he was tuning out a conversation that he should be paying attention to.

"By the time we got to Vegas, Chaos was long gone." Romulus was saying.

"So what is the plan when we do finally catch up to one of these jerks?" Hadley asked. "I mean, are we going to kill them?"

"We can't." Dorian told her. "Angels, even fallen angels cannot be killed. There is only one person who can bend their will."

"The Creator?" Thatcher asked through the momentary silence.

Dorian nodded his head and exchanged a look with the other Virtues. Thatcher suddenly felt extremely overwhelmed; no one had had a conversation with the Creator in hundreds of years. If the Creator was the only one who could stop the Maladies, how could they hope to do anything? As soon as he began to question their ability to put an end to the terrors brought on by the Maladies, he felt his anger swell.

"This is ridiculous. How are we supposed to do anything? We've been given this big mission and we've all paid dearly to be members of this exclusive club, but now we can't even do anything to stop them?" Thatcher stood up.

Shocked by his sudden outburst, the rest of the Evolved, the Virtues and Keira looked at him for a long moment before anyone spoke.

"I agree with you Thatcher. It's unfair. We haven't been appropriately prepared for many of the challenges we are facing. I'm upset by it too. But none of those feelings change the way I feel about fulfilling my purpose." Tahlia said in a shaky voice.

"You're right. I'm sorry. I'm just ready to put a stop to all this." Thatcher told her.

Thatcher thought for a moment, did his frustration change anything? Did the anger that occasionally swelled within him cause him to lose faith? He realized he couldn't even answer that question. What he really needed was answers, and the only way he was going to get any answers was to talk to the Creator face to face.

"What do we have to do to get an audience with the Creator?" Thatcher asked them.

Everyone stared at him with blank faces.

"We haven't seen or spoken with the Creator since the night he gave us the prophecies." Romulus told him patiently.

"I know that, but we have to get some answers from somewhere." Thatcher told them.

No one seemed to have anything to say, so Thatcher made up his mind. He would leave. He wasn't going to sit around like a bump on a log waiting for the next attack or waiting for the next Malady to shove their nose in his business. Thatcher took Hadley's hand and pulled her up to a standing position. He gestured for her to follow him before turning to leave the room. Thatcher was relieved to feel her hand slide back into his as he made his way to the store room where they had shared their first kiss.

He turned to face Hadley, unsure of how she would react to his plan.

"I'm leaving." He told her.

A mixture of emotions passed over her face, he saw shock replaced by fear followed by hurt and concern. He waited patiently for her to speak.

"I'm going with you." She said simply.

"No, you're not. It's not safe." Thatcher told her.

"To hell with safe. I have been patient with you long enough. You can't shut me out anymore. I love you Thatcher, you're stuck with me." Hadley told him firmly.

Thatcher watched her for a moment wondering what he could possibly say to counter that argument. Her stubbornness was one of her many endearing qualities.

"I love you too. You know that don't you?" Thatcher told her.

Hadley nodded her head and leaned in to kiss him. Thatcher felt his breath catch in his chest, he hadn't allowed himself to be this close to her since he'd gone nuts. She seemed to register his hesitation because she stopped and looked directly into his eyes. He felt her fingers trace his jaw line then run through his hair. He exhaled slowly and let his body relax. Hadley stepped closer to him, pressing her body against his; she gently pulled his face down to meet hers.

He felt her breath on his lips, inviting him to surrender to her kiss. He continued to look into her eyes and saw the passion and desperation burning in them. Thatcher reached down and pulled her body even closer to his as he allowed their lips to meet. She deepened the kiss and he welcomed it fervently.

That kiss became more than a kiss as their souls seemed to merge, healing the hurt between them. Thatcher was so lost in her kiss that he lost all sense of reason and pulled her legs up to wrap them around his waist. He pushed against her as he rested her on the counter in the storage room. He came to his senses and slowly ended the kiss. He lowered her to her feet and took a step back.

He opened his eyes to see Hadley looking at him sheepishly. He grinned at her, he had lost all sense of insecurity regarding their relationship. He pulled her close for another kiss.

The door to the store room opened slowly, and Kerr appeared behind it, followed closely by Whitley and Nora. They squeezed into the store room with them, closing the door behind them. Although they had interrupted an obviously private moment, they paid no attention and showed no concern for their interruption.

"Guys, we're kind of having a private conversation here." Thatcher told them.

"Don't care." Said Whitley with a smile and a wink at them both.

"Look, whether you like it or not, we're in this together. We are the Evolved, abilities or not." Kerr told them all with a glance at Whitley.

"Thanks." Whitley said quietly.

"We know you're going to leave." Nora told Thatcher.

Thatcher didn't bother to protest, he just stood with his arms crossed waiting for the others to say their piece.

"I can't explain it but I felt the direction of our mission shift when you made the decision to leave." Kerr told him.

"So did I." Nora said.

"The bottom line is we're stronger when we're together. We can't all go, but you need to have all the facts before you leave." Kerr told him.

"What is that even supposed to mean?" Thatcher asked.

"I can't really explain it. I had a vision of sorts. It was bits of the future. Hadley and Nora have to go with you. I saw the three of you climbing up a set of crumbling stairs, and speaking to the Creator. You're going to do it, but you're not going to do it alone." Kerr told him.

Thatcher gave his friend an appraising look. He had never known Kerr's visions to be wrong. And because he had essentially been given those visions by the Creator, Thatcher had to trust that he had been shown those instances to tell them that they could be successful in this venture.

"I already told him I'm going." Hadley told the others. "I don't want to leave you Whit, but I have to do this."

Whitley smiled at her sister and nodded, ignoring the tears that had sprung to her eyes. She pulled her sister into a tight hug. Thatcher knew they would all be leaving something important behind. If Nora was joining them, she would be leaving her husband and daughter behind; with the recent revelation of Keira's future, she had to be nervous about leaving. Hadley would be leaving the sister she had recently reunited with, and Thatcher would be leaving behind the only home he had ever really known.

"When do we leave?" Nora asked.

"We leave now." Hadley said.

Thatcher looked at the other Evolved. Even after all these years it still felt foreign to him to have the support of the people standing in this tiny store room.

GROWING hope

Chapter Twenty-One: Hadley

Hadley was ready within ten minutes. She threw clothes, toiletries, granola bars and water bottles in her backpack. She knew Nora and Thatcher would do the same.

She made her way to Whitley's room to say goodbye before they left. She eased the door open to find her sister sitting on her bed reading a book

"Hey Whit." She said, dropping her bag by the door.

"Hey Had." Whitley said, patting the bed to invite her twin to sit next to her.

Hadley joined her sister on the queen size bed. She had spent countless hours staring at the navy blue walls, trying to feel closer to her sister. Whitley's room was a stark contrast to Hadley's. Her room had been simply and tastefully decorated in muted yellows and grays. Whitley had large coral flowers painted against navy blue walls.

Whitley reached over and took Hadley's hand. "I remember not too long ago you told me you were tired of having to say goodbye every time you saw me."

"Yeah, it's still true. Only this time, I know where you'll be when I come home." Hadley told her.

"You and Nora need to stay safe. You both act tough and cocky, but you have so much more to worry about now." Whitley said.

"Without a doubt." Hadley told her sister.

"You better come back. I did not pull a Lazarus just to have you trade places with me." Whitley told her firmly.

"Yes ma'am." Hadley replied.

"I'm being serious Hadley. Don't be stupid." Whitley scolded her.

"Alright, alright. I'll be a good little super hero and protect those who are weaker than me. I'll leap tall buildings in a single..." Hadley had deepened her voice and straightened her back in a super hero stance.

"Enough already!" Whitley giggled, swatting at her sister.

"Look, I get it, but if I get all mushy now, I'm never going to pull myself together to go with them." Hadley told her sister as she fought back tears.

Whitley pulled Hadley into a tight hug.

After saying her goodbyes to Whitley, Hadley headed downstairs to meet the others. She wasn't nervous at all, her only concern was what their mother would say. She knew their dad would be there that night. He had canceled everything when he found out Whitley was back and hopped on his plane with as few secret service members as possible. He would be arriving any minute.

Nora was already in the library with Thatcher. It was clear Nora had shared a tearful goodbye with her husband and daughter. They hadn't told the Old

Immortals they were leaving, so it was a surprise when the three Virtues barreled into the library behind Hadley.

"What are you thinking?" Tahlia demanded from her daughter.

"That we need to take action." Hadley replied firmly.

"But running off on some secret mission is not the way to do this. You can't just go demand an audience with the Creator." Dorian told them pleadingly.

"We're not exactly going to demand an audience with him." Nora said.

"Then what do you plan to do? Have you even thought this through?" Tahlia demanded.

The Evolved looked at each other uncomfortably, they didn't really have a concrete plan put together, but they knew they were going to succeed. Hadley wasn't sure how to answer her mother without having to admit their lack of planning.

"You don't even have a plan?!" Tahlia almost screeched the words.

"Well, it's not that so much as we know how it will end. We figured we would let the path lead us where it will to bring us to the Creator." Hadley said realizing just how stupid that sounded.

"Look, we're going. You're not. It's been settled. You were given the mission to protect us and guide us. Congratulations you did that. But how can we be expected to accomplish the things we're supposed to if you keep trying to protect us?" Thatcher asked rhetorically.

Hadley watched as the Virtues processed that information. They knew Thatcher was right; they were all adults now. They had battled unspeakable evils and come out on top. They had been touched by loss and fear and had overcome it all.

"Where are you going?" Romulus asked quietly.

"We're going to start where we received the prophecies." Hadley told them. "It seems to be the only place we've been that was directly touched by the Creator."

"That's smart. You're right Thatcher, we have done our part, but you need to understand that we are more than just the Old Immortals, we are your family. You are young, you have barely lived and we've been here for more centuries than you'd care to know." Dorian replied. "It has been our job to guide you, teach you and prepare you. Despite our desire to be part of every step of the journey, it is time for us to hand the reigns over to you. Don't leave just yet, let me get a few things."

Dorian went to the bookshelves and began grabbing books seemingly at random. Hadley glanced at Tahlia, the strain was clear on her mother's face, but she needed to keep her face clear or her heart would break. Hadley fought back tears and turned her attention back to Dorian. Hadley recognized a few of the books he began to pile up. She had read the majority of the books in the library at least once though there were a few that hadn't made much sense. Finally, Dorian pulled a book aside and reached behind it. He sighed deeply as he handed a battered book to Nora. Hadley recognized it as the book of prophecies that had been so sacred for so long. Now, Dorian was entrusting it to them. He reached behind the books another time and pulled out a stack of notebooks. Some looked to be barely holding together despite their leather binding. Hadley watched Dorian as he approached her slowly and handed half the stack to her and half to Thatcher.

"You're going to need all the information you can get if you're going to unravel the mysteries of our lives. I dare say we have simply forgotten pieces of our history. I cannot say whether that is by the Creator's design or due to the sheer number of memories we have built up during our time on this earth. I hope you will be able to learn more from these than I have." Dorian told them.

Nora shared a meaningful look with the man who raised her before she carefully placed a stack of books in her backpack. Thatcher and Hadley did the same.

"We're not happy about this. But we would rather you go knowing we're here for you no matter what." Tahlia told them.

Hadley rushed forward and hugged her mother. She whispered for her to look after Whitley and to give her love to her dad.

Thatcher shook hands with both Dorian and Romulus then gave Tahlia a quick hug. The girls gave hugs all around. Then the three of them stood in a circle and joined hands.

The library melted around them and they found themselves standing amongst the temple ruins where they had all been five years before. While the jungle around them had continued to grow, the trees still parted perfectly to allow the sun to shine on this spot. The trio took a moment to look around and reacquaint themselves with the ruins. Hadley hadn't really spent much time exploring when they had been there before.

She and her sister had discussed their prophecy at the stone table. She walked around the stone table to stand in the spot she'd been in with her mother after Whitley had stormed off.

Her life and become so full since the day they joined the Old Immortals. Thatcher came up behind her and wrapped his arms around her.

"I love you." He whispered into her ear.

"I love you too." Hadley replied contentedly.

"Alright, let's take a peek into Dorian's research shall we?" Nora said from behind them.

Hadley turned around to see her sitting on a broken piece of a column, she had started looking through the book of prophecies. Hadley took a seat across from her and grabbed the oldest of the research notebooks. She opened to the first page and began reading.

Chapter Twenty-Two: Tahlia

Eric had blown a gasket when he arrived to discover that Hadley had run off to who knows where with Thatcher and Nora. He understood why they left, he just didn't appreciate being the last to know again.

"Lia, I thought we talked about this." Eric told her. "The only way we can make this work is if there are no more secrets between us."

"I understand what you're saying and I understand why you're upset, but you need to understand that a lot of this stuff is out of my hands too. We can't exactly call a family meeting every time the Evolved decide to take off on some mission." Tahlia told him.

"I know. But when my daughter is involved I would at least like a phone call." Eric told her.

"Our daughter, and I didn't think I needed to call because you were going to be here soon." Tahlia retorted. "Anyway, our other daughter is excited to see her father."

Eric had given Tahlia a torn look, it was still too much to hope that Whitley was back. Tahlia would never have put Eric through this if she weren't certain they had their baby back. She took his hand and led him to the kitchen where Whitley was waiting with freshly baked cookies.

"Hi daddy!" Whitley squealed as she flew into his arms.

Eric choked back a sob as he held the daughter he thought he lost. Tahlia wrapped her arms around both of them.

"Oh baby, I thought you were gone." Eric told Whitley with tears streaming down his face.

"I was only gone for a little while. I'm sorry you guys had to go through all that." Whitley told him trying to make him feel better.

"It's not your fault sweetie. You did what I asked you to. You protected your sister.

You saw that she was in danger and you acted without question." Eric told.

Whitley reached up and wiped the tears from her father's cheeks and gently kissed the last spot the tears had rested.

"Come on, I made cookies!" Whitley said cheerfully.

Tahlia and Eric sat down and grabbed an oatmeal butterscotch cookie.

"So, you did it huh? You're Mr. President." Whitley teased her father.

"Well, yes. It's an election year though, so we don't know for sure that I'll be re-elected." Eric told her.

"Oh please Eric, don't be so modest. You're father has been doing a great job in his role, one of the most-loved presidents to lead our country in as many years." Tahlia replied glowing with pride.

"Glad to hear it. And you two? When are you getting remarried?" Whitley asked bluntly.

Eric started choking on his cookie. Tahlia reached up and smacked him on the back with all her might. He coughed a few times before regaining his composure.

"We haven't really talked about that." Tahlia offered.

"That's not true. We've talked about it, but your mother doesn't want to get married until she finds out if she's going to die." Eric replied.

"What?" Whitley looked at her mother in surprise.

Tahlia kicked Eric under the table. She shot him a warning look, but it was too late. Tahlia knew Whitley wouldn't let that comment go without exploring every possible angle.

"Mother?" She asked, her tone indicating she was demanding an answer.

"I don't know what's going to happen with the Maladies and I don't want to break your father's heart twice." Tahlia said simply.

"Besides, we're practically still married anyway."

"Mother!" Whitley exclaimed turning red.

"Oh please." Tahlia replied.

"At any rate, I plan to make an honest woman out of your mother as soon as all this business with the Maladies is sorted out." Eric said with a warm smile at Tahlia.

"Well that's a relief." Whitley said.

Whitley smiled at her parents before excusing herself to take cookies to Keira and Kerr who had built a fort in the backyard.

"She's really back?" Eric asked.

"She's really back. I don't know entirely why, but I have a feeling we'll find out eventually. Right now, I'm just thankful. You should have seen them together again." Tahlia told Eric.

"I'll see it soon enough. Hadley will be back as soon as she figures out whatever she's decided to figure out." Eric replied.

Tahlia knew he was right, she just didn't know when they would see Hadley again. Whitley breezed back in the door with Kerr and Keira trailing behind her.

"Well there's a little princess who needs a hug!" Eric said as he lifted Keira into his arms.

"Hi Eric!" Keira said as she hugged him around the neck.

Tahlia smiled at the sight of Eric holding the little girl.

Tahlia couldn't help but feel the ache in her belly that told her she would give anything to have another child. Eric had continued to age and was now in his mid-forties, but Tahlia was still suspended as a thirty-something woman in the prime of her life. She knew that if they did find a way to move to the next step in mending their damaged relationship that they could have another baby. Tahlia wasn't sure how Eric or the girls would feel about that considering the insanity that surrounded their lives, but she wanted to hold on to that glimmer of possibility for a little longer.

"I have an idea!" Whitley said startling Tahlia from her thoughts.

"What's that sweetheart?" Her father asked.

"Let's go for ice cream in Benton." Whitley said with a mischievous smile.

They decided to take Keira with them to allow Kerr some time to talk to Romulus and Dorian. When they arrived at the Dairy Barn they piled out of Eric's armored car after the secret service agents established that it was safe. What a surprise for the people of Benton; they knew he occasionally returned home to visit, but he rarely wandered in to town.

They ordered their ice cream from the stunned manager. He was a friendly young man, and Tahlia was certain that if it weren't for his ebony skin his face would have flushed red as he bustled around to ensure that the President had everything he needed.

They took their ice cream to go and decided to take a walk along the path at Riverside Park. Eric held her hand as they walked watching Whitley chase Keira along the way. It was a beautiful day, one of the last they would see before the winter months came.

"Mom!" Whitley called out to her a second too late.

Strong hands grabbed her from behind and roughly pulled her away from Eric. She tried to fight against them, but she was powerless to resist. Everything happened so quickly, she was in the clutches of an unknown enemy, then a shot rang out and she saw Eric fall from the corner of her eye. A scream tore from her chest.

Chapter Twenty-Three: Kerr

Saying goodbye to Nora without knowing when he may see her again had been the hardest thing he had ever done. When Tahlia and Eric volunteered to take Keira with them for ice cream, Kerr was more than happy to agree. He wanted some time to talk to Romulus about the other Evolved.

"I can't explain it Romulus. I just know that somehow, they're going to do it." Kerr told him.

"The Creator has truly blessed you with a gift. Those visions of yours have helped us immensely." Romulus told him. "You get them more often than I ever did"

Kerr smiled at him. He knew the Old Immortal held no jealousy in his heart even though he had every reason to envy his descendant. Kerr had been lucky enough to find the love of his life and keep her while Romulus had had to deal with losing his soul mate with the birth of his son. He sat with Romulus in silence. They had grown comfortable enough with each other that they didn't have to verbally communicate in order to understand each other.

Kerr felt a searing pain rip through his stomach without warning. He gasped and reached down to grab the spot where the pain had radiated from. He brought his hand back and saw it was covered in blood. Romulus gave him a look that said everything Kerr himself was thinking, then the room went black.

He stood in the middle of Riverside Park. His abdomen no longer hurt, but he saw the original source of the pain. Eric lay face down on the ground, blood pooling around him. The secret service agents lay less than twenty feet from him. Kerr walked closer to them and discovered they appeared to be covered in ugly pustules. Their lifeless eyes stared at the sky, frozen in the shock of the disease that claimed their lives.

Kerr felt panic begin to rise in his chest as he scanned the area looking for his daughter. Had the Maladies discovered that she was likely the next vessel to be chosen by the spirit of hope?

He looked around desperately, but couldn't find Whitley or Keira. Tahlia was missing too.

He knelt by Eric, he was dead.

Kerr opened his eyes to find Dorian and Romulus staring at him. He quickly looked down and patted his stomach, checking for blood. The only blood he found was the blood that had dried on his hand from the initial pain he had before the vision.

"We need to go. Now." Kerr told them.

"I'll stay in case you need something." Dorian said.

He took a chance and called out for Nora, praying she would answer his call. She materialized next to him and registered the desperation in his eyes within seconds. He felt Romulus grab onto him just before Nora whisked them away.

Nora dropped them off and left to get Hadley and Thatcher. They knew there was a possibility that they'd be called back during their journey, at least they had the luxury of being able to travel instantly from one place to another.

Kerr pointed to the secret service agents that lay on the ground then ran towards Eric. If he hurried, he might be able to heal him. He fell to his knees and felt the man's neck. He was relieved to feel a faint and slow pulse. As long as there was a pulse, he could heal him.

"Eric!" Kerr said, rolling him over as gently as he could. "Eric, you need to wake up."

The man wouldn't wake and his pulse grew weaker and slower until it stopped. Kerr had failed.

Hadley appeared next to him and gripped her father's shoulders.

"No. This cannot happen." She said through gritted teeth.

Hadley rubbed her hands together, energy crackled between them. She looked at Kerr for a moment before steeling herself for what was to come. She placed her crackling hands on Eric's chest. She was a human defibrillator. She delivered a shock to his heart, then waited a few moments. When nothing happened, she leaned forward and shocked him again. He took an involuntary breath. She had managed to restart his heart.

"Daddy! Wake up. Wake up!" She yelled at him and smacked his face.

Kerr watched her pull back to deliver another shock to him but grabbed her hand when Eric's eyes fluttered open. He instantly set to work trying to heal the bullet wound in his abdomen.

"The bullet is still in there. I've never healed something like this. I can heal the area where the pain is, and heal what is causing the pain, but I can't remove the bullet. It needs to come out." Kerr said evenly.

Hadley smacked his hand away and wordlessly held her own hand over the wound. Eric cried out from the pain. Kerr watched her hand hover there and was sufficiently impressed when the bullet flew out of Eric's stomach and into her hand.

"Magnetic pull." Hadley shrugged at him.

Kerr went back to work on healing the wound. The green light wrapped itself around Eric's body, growing steadily brighter until it dissipated in a flash.

"Thank you." Eric said. He sat up suddenly, seeming to remember that he had not been alone in the park.

"Your men are dead." Kerr told him sadly. "The Maladies turned them against you, then killed them."

"And we can't find mom, Whitley or Keira." Hadley told him.

Eric stood and looked around him. Kerr knew without asking that he hadn't seen who had attacked them and was just as clueless as they were regarding the location of the others.

"We're going to have to talk to the police. These men are dead, and I'm sure people heard the gun shot. What are we going to tell them?" Eric asked them.

As if on cue, the sirens became audible and drew closer to them. They quickly discussed their story, deciding that Romulus would stay with Eric and the rest of them should leave. The fewer there were to question, the quicker they could find the rest of the family.

Chapter Twenty-Four: Whitley

"Keira, where are we?" Whitley asked the little girl uncertainly.

Just moments ago they had witnessed her father being shot by one of his own men and Tahlia being dragged off by another. Now, they were standing in the middle of the park all alone.

"We're in the other place." Keira told her as though that explained everything.

Whitley looked around and realized the muted colors and silence were exactly the same as the place she had been wandering looking for a way to get back to the house.

"What is this place?" Whitley asked.

"I don't know. I'm just a kid." Keira told her.

"Well aren't you a little sassy pants?" Whitley asked her rhetorically.

Keira took Whitley's hand and pointed to the river. A woman stood there by the water. She turned to look at them and raised her hand to wave at Whitley.

"Lida!" Whitley cried out as she ran to her.

Lida embraced her warmly. Whitley didn't think she would ever see this Old Immortal again after she was given her life back.

"Hello dear girl. And hello to you Miss Mason." Lida said with a bright smile at Keira.

"I don't understand, what are you doing here? What are we doing here?" Whitley asked Lida. "We need to go back, my mom and dad need us."

"Your father is being cared for." Lida told her.

The way she hadn't mentioned her mother told Whitley something was wrong. She waited for Lida to offer an explanation but one didn't come.

"As far as what you're doing here, it is time we met Keira." Lida said gently.

"Why do you wanna meet me?" She asked.

"Well, you have been tapping in to our collective abilities. Some of them are going to be very useful in the coming days." Lida told her.

"What is that supposed to mean Lida?" Whitley demanded. "What happened to my mother?"

Lida smiled at her kindly, but Whitley could detect a hint of sorrow in that smile. "Your mother has been taken by the Maladies. They mean to destroy her."

"We need to go help her!" Whitley said urgently.

"Your mother will live. She has served the Creator faithfully all these years. The more pressing issue is that they will succeed in extracting the spirit of hope from her." Lida told them.

Whitley looked at Keira with concern. If they were going to extract the spirit from her mother, wouldn't that put the little girl in danger? How could the Creator expect such an innocent person to carry such a heavy weight?

"We hadn't planned on this happening for years. With the death of Absalom, the Maladies have grown braver and much more reckless. Keira wasn't supposed to come into her role as the vessel until she was older." Lida shared.

"How do they plan to 'extract' the spirit of hope from my mother?" Whitley asked, afraid of the answer.

"We don't know. We just know we need to prepare the next vessel." Lida said, placing a hand on Keira's shoulder.

Whitley couldn't believe what she was hearing. How could they see some things but not all? How did they know her mother would live? How did they know the Maladies would succeed in extracting the spirit of hope from Tahlia? Whitley was so frustrated she couldn't even find the words to express her feelings.

"It will all turn out alright." Lida told her. "For now, we have a few things to discuss with you Keira."

Whitley sat down and pulled Keira into her lap. The little girl began playing with Whitley's long golden hair while she leaned her head on her shoulder.

"Keira, your mother and the other Evolved are searching for a way to get into this plane. You are the only one who can help them. You have been able to come here out of desperation and fear, but I will give you the ability to come here at will. That is the only way they will be able to find our home and the Creator." Lida told her.

"But I don't really know how we come here. I didn't meant to. I was just scared." Keira told her.

"I know dear one, but soon, you will just need to knock and the door will open for you." Lida whispered.

"What is this place?" Whitley asked Lida, unsure if she would receive an answer.

"You are in a realm that exists outside of time. It is simply your world but a different plane of existence. This is the realm where the Creator lives, this is the realm where the Council of Immortals lived before we were banished for mating with humans."

"But what do we call it?" Keira asked Lida curiously.

"This is Eternity." Lida replied simply. "All souls pass through here on their journey to the light or damnation. This is where your daddy goes in his visions but he has a special ability to see both realms at once."

Whitley noticed that Keira was paying close attention to everything Lida said. Something inside this little girl was ready to learn everything and take on all the responsibility that would be hers when the Maladies had finished with Tahlia.

"Are you ready to learn?" Lida asked Keira.

The little girl nodded eagerly. Lida leaned forward and kissed her forehead gently. A blinding light surrounded them as Lida transferred her power to the small child before her.

"You have now been granted all the knowledge that will prepare you for what lies ahead." Lida told her.

"Thank you Lida. Whitley, let's go help your mommy." Keira told her.

Whitley let Keira take her hand and soon found herself standing in the park in the real world. There were bodies all around them, but relief flooded through her when she saw her father talking to a police officer with Romulus nearby.

"Daddy!" She yelled as she began running in to his arms.

"Whitley! Where have you been baby? I was so worried. Oh and Keira. Where did you guys go?" Eric said as tears ran down his face and into her hair.

"Dad, we don't have a lot of time. We need to get to mom. She's alive, but they're going to do something to her." Whitley whispered to him.

She now knew that the secret service agents who had attacked her parents had been working under the influence of the Maladies. For all she knew, one of the men lying dead on the ground around them had been the one who pulled the trigger.

Her mother was gone, but they would get her back. She would be alive but only the Creator knew what shape she would be in.

Chapter Twenty-Five: Tahlia

Shortly after being tossed unceremoniously into the back of a van, Tahlia was blindfolded and knocked unconscious. The last thing that was burned in her mind was seeing Eric lying on the ground as the life oozed out of him. That had also been the first thing she remembered when she awoke.

She knew who had taken her. She knew the Maladies had finally found a way to get her away from her family. She didn't know what had become of her daughter or Keira during the attack, but Tahlia said a silent prayer that they had gotten away.

Tahlia took a deep breath and instantly wished she hadn't. The stench of Disease filled the air around her.

"Hey Crusty, where are we going?" Tahlia taunted, hoping he could hear her.

"Shut-up." She heard the scratchy voice reply.

"No thanks." Tahlia replied.

"Go ahead and let her talk. It's not like she has much time left anyway." The steely voice of Malice said from the darkness.

The van came to a rough stop and she was pulled from the now open door. Her blindfold was ripped off, taking some of her hair with it. She hated that her eyes watered from the sudden sting of her hair being ripped out.

She took the opportunity to look around her. Her heart fell when she saw that all the Maladies had graced her with their presence. They wouldn't have gathered all together if they weren't planning something big. She looked around her and found she was in an abandoned out building. She didn't know how long they'd driven while she was unconscious, but she hoped she wasn't too far from home. There was sunlight streaming down from the ceiling, she looked up to see a hole blasted from the inside out. Her stomach clenched as she made the connection between this location and the very place Malcolm had been tortured and nearly killed before their battle with Absalom. She looked back at the Maladies with a steely resolve.

Chaos winked at her. The young woman looked like your average teenager with her pink and purple pixie cut and nose ring. She wore torn up jeans and a patchwork halter top. Next to her was Avarice; she looked like she had everything together. Her perfectly highlighted honey blonde hair was pulled neatly into a pony tail at the base of her neck, not a hair out of place. Her narrow blue eyes and turned up nose gave the impression of a snotty soccer mom.

Vanity and Panic stood behind Avarice. Pain was crouched near the ground, and next to him stood Rage. Tahlia knew she had been brought to that place by Malice and Disease, they were standing next to her.

"What's this all about guys?" Tahlia asked, trying to sound nonchalant.

Malice came to stand in front of her, leaning right into her face. "We're going to snuff out that light you've been shining around all these years."

"Unfortunately we've discovered that we can't infect you by touching you the way we have with the humans and your precious Evolved. Disease did his best while you were sleeping." Rage told her.

Tahlia didn't want to know what that meant. She prayed she would never find out what had happened while she'd been knocked out.

"Even though we can't infect you, we can torture you. We can rip the spirit of hope right out of you, and then, we can kill you." Malice whispered.

"You can try." Tahlia said in a steady voice.

"I'm looking forward to this." Said Pain.

They dragged her to a chair and slammed her into it. Soon her arms and legs were bound and she steeled herself for what would come next.

"While Malice and Pain do their thing, I'm going to tell you a story." Rage told her.

"Thanks, I'm not in the mood for story time." Tahlia told him.

Malice slapped her hard across the face. Chaos laughed and Avarice stuck her nose even higher up in the air as though the whole situation made her feel dirty.

"Once upon a time, there were some good little angels who did everything they were asked. They watched over the world and helped the Creator guide each of his creations as per his plan. But then the Creator decided he wasn't done. He made a special group of beings who were allowed to interact with his most precious creation, man." Rage began his story, each word dripping with disdain and anger.

Malice knelt in front of her and slowly pushed a pin under the nail of her index finger. Tahlia did her best not to cry out but the pain was so intense, she let a small gasp escape her.

"Now, Tahlia, it's rude to interrupt a man when he's telling you a story." Rage scolded her like a child.

"My apologies. Please continue." Tahlia said in a measured tone.

"Some of these angels wanted to help with those precious creations. But the Creator wouldn't have it. He said no. So, they had no other choice, they went behind his back. They decided man was too clean. Man was too 'perfect'. And these Immortals that had been created to guide them were just too loving." Rage paused as Malice pushed another pin under her middle finger nail.

This time Tahlia had braced herself for the pain. She didn't make a sound.

"Just when they were starting to make life more interesting for man, the Creator discovered what they were doing. And this loving and benevolent Creator banished them. He didn't just strip them of their angel status, he banished them to the deepest darkest chasm he could find. He stuffed them into a hole and locked them away so they couldn't mess up his perfect world." Rage continued as a pin drove under the fingernail of her ring finger.

"All pretense aside, I'm sure you know that those angels are now standing around you. But we weren't always like this. Oh no, the Creator did more than just banish us. He ensured that we would not be able to hide our true nature ever again. We took on the semblance of our 'sins'. Some of us got off pretty easy, some of us, well..." Rage gestured at Pain and Disease.

Despite the pain she was in, Tahlia felt like antagonizing him a bit more. She knew that whether she kept quiet or taunted the Maladies, her torture would continue.

"You think you got off easy? I can practically see the fury dripping from your sweaty brow. And Malice here, well, she looks like a total bitch. Vanity looks like a slutty cheerleader. Avarice honey, you constantly look as though you're smelling something foul, and I'm sure it's not just Disease. Panic could easily pass for a strung out coke head and Pain is just hideously disfigured." Tahlia paused briefly to take a breath. "The only one who looks semi-decent is Chaos. But it's not like she really affects that many people."

Now she'd done it. She watched Rage's nostrils flare. His face had always reminded her of a snake. He had strange wide set eyes that looked red when the light hit them. His nose was wide, but the nostrils were narrow. Tahlia wasn't sure if his tendency to over-annunciate the letter 's' was natural or a testament to his snake like features. Avarice stepped forward and slapped Tahlia across the face hard enough that her head jerked to the left with the impact.

"Right now, the only foul thing I smell is you Tahlia. You have no idea who you're dealing with." Avarice told her haughtily.

Tahlia hissed in pain as a sharp razor sliced across her arm. She looked over to see Pain smiling in wicked glee. It took everything in her not to let them see her discomfort through tears, she knew this was only the beginning.

"So, anyway, I'll pick up where you left off." Chaos told Rage. "Many strange things happened in the Underworld as you can imagine. It was like a place out of time. We began absorbing the souls of those who had committed the very sins we were being punished for. It was actually kind of cool. That Dante guy didn't get it completely right, there aren't really nine circles of hell. There are eight of us, and the souls of the damned don't exactly go through tortures so much as hang out with others like themselves."

"So you have some kind of support group?" Tahlia asked.

"Don't be silly Tahlia. The Creator thought he was punishing us while helping us see the error in our ways. He had intended for us to live out eternity amongst the souls of those who had committed sins similar to our own, I believe he hoped it would show us the light." Chaos laughed harshly.

"What he must not have realized is that he was feeding us. He was sending those dark souls down to us to add to our collection of depravity."

Tahlia was beginning to connect the dots. The Creator thought he could help his angels by showing them others who had suffered terrible fates as a result of their treachery. Somehow, these monsters in front of her had found a way to circumvent the Creator's will and twist their punishment to benefit their evil deeds.

Pain proceeded to make small slices along the top of her breasts. She hadn't even noticed that they'd ripped her shirt. She tried desperately to separate herself from the pain they were inflicting, but just as she'd gain control, Malice would stick another pin under a fingernail. Her hands felt like they were on fire, the tender nerves were expressing their protest by shooting pain up from her finger tips to her shoulders.

"Why are you telling me all this?" Tahlia asked them angrily.

"We have our reasons." Malice said through her teeth.

"Mostly because no one has taken the time to listen to us since Absalom. That was a great day. We still don't know how long we were truly trapped down there, but one fine day someone literally burned a hole in the rocks that acted as our prison. We were suddenly free. But this man with these special powers intrigued us, we had never been given abilities of any kind." Chaos said with a hint of regret.

"Absalom freed us, and in return, we told him our story. I think he had been waiting for someone to validate the feelings that had been creeping up on him slowly. He took what we told him and built a plan. A masterful plan. He became a double agent so to speak." Rage said.

"He wanted more than what the Creator had given him. He wanted to be more powerful. He wanted to rally an army that would follow him. We wanted to be by his side when he did." Avarice shared, it was clear that the idea of all that power affected her.

"So you teamed up with Absalom. I already know he trapped you in the golden sphere, obviously he betrayed you." Tahlia said breathlessly, the torture was beginning to break her resolve.

"No dear, he didn't betray us. That was part of the plan. What you don't understand is that the Creator had left us to rot in hell but he had taken precautions to ensure that we could not approach man ever again. Man couldn't even see us. We couldn't touch him. We weren't corporeal. We couldn't leave the realm the Creator had created." Rage told her slowly.

"The day we went with Absalom to meet the Council of Immortals and face our Creator once more, we already knew we would be stuffed into that wretched ball. The only possible way for us to have any effect on humans was for a human to allow us to enter the world once more." Chaos said, watching something over Tahlia's shoulder with great interest.

An icy torrent flowed over her body as Pain and Malice took turns pouring ice cold water over her. She shivered when the first wave stopped, her teeth chattering together. She heard them behind her again and braced herself for the cold water. Instead, she was hit with boiling water that seared her skin and left her feeling the sting all over her body. They repeated this sequence in silence three more times. Tahlia could feel the blisters forming all over her skin.

Tahlia couldn't take the pain much longer, her body was begging for respite. Her mind seemed to give in as the room grew darker before her and the voices faded away to silence.

Chapter Twenty-Six: Dorian

Relief flooded through him when Romulus came through the door carrying a sleeping Keira in his arms. Whitley followed close behind with her father.

"Where have you been?" Hadley demanded from her sister.

"We were in Eternity." Whitley said.

Eternity. The word was like a trigger for something buried deep inside his soul. Dorian looked at Romulus to find his confusion mirrored in his brothers face. Eternity. Hearing the word was like a sweet song that called to him on his deepest level of existence.

"You don't remember it do you?" Whitley asked them both quietly.

"I don't know. I can feel that it means something to me." Dorian replied as he tried to grasp the memory.

"Eternity is your home silly Papa!" Keira giggled, she must have awoken at the sound of their conversation.

The memories flooded back to him. He had known they had lived in many places throughout their lives, but he had forgotten that they were all one place. His home had remained unchanged and protected throughout his entire existence. He recalled the large mountain that towered over them. He remembered entering at the base of the mountain that was really a vast multi-level city built just for the Council of Immortals, angels and the Creator.

"Eternity." Romulus said, the realization was evident in his voice.

"But why wouldn't you remember it?" Thatcher asked them.

"They couldn't." Keira told them sadly. "They weren't allowed to go back because they were no longer pure of heart."

All heads swiveled in her direction. Her sweet voice seemed to hold a knowledge within it that belied her innocence. Kerr gently took his daughter from Romulus and looked into her eyes.

"What does that mean sweet pea?" Kerr asked her curiously.

"They had babies with girls. God didn't like that." Keira said.

Dorian met Romulus' eyes and saw the pain and regret etched in his features. They had known that mating with human women had been a pivotal moment in their existence, but they had forgotten it was the reason they had been banished to live amongst humans instead of staying with the Creator. Their sins had been the reason for not only the division amongst the Old Immortals but also for their separation from the Creator himself.

"When we were identified as the Virtues by the Creator, we realized that he was giving us the opportunity to atone for our sins. Despite the Creator not supporting what we had done, he saw a future purpose for the children we had created. By having children, we had unknowingly created the only weakness our race had ever seen. But, because the Creator saw that most of us were repentant, our ancestors would also be the greatest asset the world had in putting an end to the evil Absalom had brought to the world. Sadly, we knew we would eventually be left with only five descendants as per the prophecies we received." Dorian told them with a mixture of pride and shame.

"Do you remember anything else about Eternity?" Nora asked them.

"It's been so long." Romulus told them.

"I can only remember bits and pieces. I do remember though that the Creator lived at the top of the mountain. The Great Hall was his home." Dorian told them.

They were silent for a few moments. Dorian pushed aside thoughts of Eternity in order to bring the focus back to Tahlia. She was still missing.

"Any clue as to where Tahlia is?" Dorian asked Whitley.

"The Maladies. They took her. I'm guessing they infected the secret service guys while we were getting our ice cream. I saw someone grab mom and drag her away." Whitley told them.

"Nora have you been able to sense her?" Kerr asked his wife.

Nora shook her head sadly. "It's like a radio station that comes in and out. As soon as I think I feel her, there's nothing there. I don't know what that means, it's just...."

Nora stopped talking and sat up straight like she was listening to something. She slumped down again and shrugged. "It's like she's blocking me or something."

"If Tahlia is blocking you, she's doing it for good reason." Romulus told them.

"But I can only imagine what they may be doing to her." Hadley whispered as Thatcher pulled her close.

"They can't kill her right?" Thatcher asked with a guilty look at Romulus.

"She won't die." Keira told them simply.

It was unnerving for Keira to speak in such a way. He wasn't sure what had happened to her in Eternity, but it had clearly affected her. He was about to ask Whitley for some guidance when she offered it on her own.

"It was Lida. She kissed Keira's forehead and shared some special knowledge with her. She told us they hadn't expected this to happen for a long time. She said that they have to..." Whitley broke off with a nervous glance at Nora and Kerr.

"They have to what Whit?" Hadley asked her, reaching over to take Nora's hand.

"They have to prepare the next vessel." Whitley finished.

Dorian knew then that their conjectures had been correct. Keira was indeed to be the next vessel for the spirit of hope. "So they're going to try to get the spirit to leave Tahlia?"

Whitley nodded. "If it leaves her, it will go to the new vessel."

"So Keira will be their next target?" Nora asked in fear.

"They don't know about me mommy." Keira said hugging her mother's leg.

This was a new development. If the Maladies didn't know a new vessel had already been chosen, they planned to release the spirit of hope and watch it fade away. Without a new vessel, hope would die. Once again, the Creator had proven that he would plan ahead to protect the world.

"If we have any hope of defeating them, we need to figure out what we're going to do with them. We don't have a special golden sphere to stuff them into. So we need to figure something else out." Thatcher said.

Dorian nodded in agreement. "I think we need to send them back to the underworld."

Everyone seemed to understand that it was time for them to separate once again. Nora bade farewell to her husband and daughter, Hadley and Thatcher said their goodbyes to those who would stay behind and search for Tahlia. Dorian pulled each of them into a tight hug just before they disappeared from the sitting room.

Chapter Twenty-Seven: Tahlia

Tahlia woke to find herself in a completely different place. Had she been rescued? Had they moved her just to mess with her head? She looked around to see she was lying on the ground in a field. The sky overhead was clear and blue with pure white clouds dotted all over. Tahlia rolled over and realized the pain was gone.

She wondered briefly if they had managed to kill her somehow. Tahlia looked down at her clothes to see herself wearing a long simple maxi dress. She stood slowly and looked around, wondering what she would find.

"Hello Tahlia." A voice said behind her.

She turned at the sound to find herself face to face with Charis. The Old Immortal had been her best friend for centuries. Tahlia smiled and rushed into her friend's waiting embrace.

"Where am I?" She asked as she pulled away.

"You're unconscious in the real world, but we were able to pull you into Eternity for now." Charis told her.

"Us? Where are the others?" She asked glancing around hopefully.

"It's just me right now." Charis said taking Tahlia's hand in hers.

"Why am I here? They didn't kill me did they?" Tahlia asked desperately.

There was too much riding on her survival for them to have succeeded so quickly.

"No. They've been doing their best, but you are not going to die at their hands." Charis told her gently. "I do need to prepare you though. It's time for you to learn where you came from."

Tahlia perked up at her words. Unlike the story the Maladies were telling her during the hours of torture, this was a tale she longed to hear.

"Come with me Tahlia." Charis said as she led her across the field.

They were heading towards a shack sitting on its own in the middle of nowhere. As they neared, Tahlia heard muffled cries coming from within.

"This isn't going to be easy for you, but it is necessary for you to know who you were and why you became the first vessel." Charis said quietly. "You are going to see visions of your past. You're going to see everything."

Tahlia nodded and followed Charis around the shack, she didn't pause when Charis walked straight through the door. When she arrived in the small room the first thing she saw was a woman in labor. The woman stood on two bricks with her legs spread to shoulder width. She pushed and struggled as she leaned against the wall for leverage; she was all alone.

Tahlia looked at her face and felt sorry for the pain the woman was enduring. There was no husband to be seen; no one to make sure she was alright.

"Who is she?" Tahlia asked Charis.

"She is your mother." She replied.

Tahlia looked at the woman again and saw the shape of her face and sweaty blond hair. Her mother. She didn't remember her, she didn't remember anything. Tahlia tried not to let her frustration interrupt this moment.

Her mother screamed in agony and pushed until her face turned beet red. The ragged breaths filled the space and left her with little strength for the final push. Tahlia watched in wonder as her mother leaned forward and pushed once more; she reached down to catch the small baby with one hand. Using the other to hold herself steady.

She took a few moments to catch her breath after her labor before looking at the babe in her hand. She stepped down from the bricks and gingerly pulled a knife from the counter to cut the cord that hung from inside her. Once the cord was severed, she set the baby on the table.

Tahlia looked at Charis in concern. The baby still hadn't cried. It looked still. She watched her mother as she finished cleaning herself up and packed some cloth below her dress to slow the bleeding. Her mother turned to look at the baby and a small moment of indecision crossed her face. She turned her back on the child and began cleaning the mess from the floor.

"What is she doing?" Tahlia asked. "Why isn't she concerned about the baby?"

"Wait." Charis instructed.

The child stirred. The baby who was Tahlia cried. She sucked in air and let out a shrill scream, her body shaking from the sudden realization that her surroundings had changed.

Tahlia looked between the baby and mother, waiting as Charis had instructed. Her mother leaned against a counter with hunched shoulders, her back to the baby.

Tahlia's heart broke thinking about how lonely and terrible her first moments in this world had been. She didn't understand why her mother refused to comfort the baby lying on the table.

Her mother turned around to face the child she'd birthed a few moments ago. Tahlia saw the look of fear and torment on the woman's face. She held her hands over her ears as tears fell down her face. As she put her hands down she looked at the child and her resolve melted.

Tahlia watched as her mother carefully picked the baby up from the table and looked at her. The fear and torment was quickly replaced by awe and love. She went to the cot in the corner and held her daughter close, nursing her as she lay on the small bed.

"Your mother did not want a child." Charis told her softly. "She had been raped at fifteen. She was alone in the world, no family, no money and no hope. But then she let herself love you and her life changed."

Tahlia watched as time seemed to speed around them. The baby grew to a toddler, then to a girl, and finally to a young woman before everything slowed down again. Her mother had aged gracefully and stood brushing her daughter's hair in the small shack.

Tahlia felt the warmth and love in the small home. She smiled at the way her mother looked at her; it was so much like the way she looked at her own daughters. Time sped past them again leaving Tahlia and Charis alone in the decrepit home.

"It can't have simply been the change I brought about in my mother that led the spirit of hope to choose me as the vessel." Tahlia said slowly. "What happens next?"

"Your mother contracted a deadly illness and died when you were barely a woman." Charis said softly. "You had no one, you had no money. You were in much the same predicament as your mother."

The scene around them melted away and Tahlia found herself standing in a crowded marketplace. She looked around trying to determine what she should be looking at when she was startled by another voice.

"Tahlia." A deep rumbling voice said behind her.

She turned to find Lucien standing behind her. She stepped into his warm embrace. "My dear brother, it's been so long."

"That it has. Are you ready to learn more?" Lucien asked kindly.

"Ready as I'll ever be I'm sure." She told him with a wry smile.

He pointed to a doorway covered by a ragged curtain. They closed the space between it and them quickly and were soon inside the dark structure. Tahlia looked around at the room they stood in. There were beds separated by curtains; some of the curtains were drawn and she heard muffled sounds come from behind them. She exchanged a look with Lucien that she hoped told him she didn't want to know why they were there.

A man burst into the room from another door dragging a young girl behind him, her blonde hair flying wildly as she fought him. He threw her into the room and struck her to the ground. Tahlia watched in horror as the man kicked her in the stomach. Her younger self cried and held onto her swollen midsection. She was pregnant. Tahlia looked to Lucien to find him nodding gravely at her and indicating that she should continue to observe.

The young girl begged him to stop as he beat her mercilessly. When he was done, she lay in a pool of blood on the floor. An older woman came and took her to another room where loud screams of agony erupted from the young girl.

"I was with child." Tahlia said in shock.

"You had hidden it from your master as long as you could. When he discovered your secret, you were no good to him unless you were unburdened. He put an end to your pregnancy in those moments." Lucien said sadly.

"Was I a prostitute?" Tahlia asked against the lump in her throat.

"More like a consort or concubine. You belonged to this man and his brother. You and two other young women." Lucien said as he gestured to the closed off area behind them.

"Why did he kill his own child? If I was only for him and his brother, why would he do that?" Tahlia asked, devastated by what she'd witnessed.

"Wives were for childbearing, consorts were for pleasure. He did not need or want another child. He wanted sex." Lucien replied.

Tahlia couldn't believe the direction her life had taken. She'd changed her mother's life but ended up in an existence filled with abuse and torment. She'd had a child cruelly stolen from her and hadn't even remembered.

Time sped again, Tahlia witnessed her master use and abuse her over the years.

She saw her masters beat her and allow her to be nursed back to health so they could find pleasure in her again. She was about to ask Lucien why she had to see all this when he placed a hand on her arm and gestured towards the battered young woman who had been Tahlia in another life.

She watched with interest as the young Tahlia ground something with a mortar and pestle before mixing it into two drinks. She was standing in the room alone with no clothing on. She was waiting for someone. When both masters arrived she smiled at them. She handed each a drink and stood before them as they drank and leered at her nudity. Tahlia felt her stomach turn at the way they watched her.

Soon both men began to choke. They turned red and scratched at their throats. All the while, the younger Tahlia stood before them with a smile on her face. When both men stopped moving, she took the glasses and rinsed them in a bucket of water. Then she screamed.

The old woman who had taken her away after her beating arrived and began yelling at Tahlia. It was clear she would not get away with this. Time sped up to Tahlia standing before a crowd with stones in their hands, tears fell down her cheeks as she waited for the first stone to be thrown.

Thankfully, Lucien did not make her watch her own execution. She closed her eyes and turned away, unable to bear the thought of what would come next. When she opened her eyes again she stood in the bright field once more.

"I murdered them." Tahlia said.

"You were with child again." Lucien told her.

"What?" Tahlia asked in shock.

"You had discovered your pregnancy but had still not shown signs. Rather than let them take your child from you again, you killed them." Lucien told her.

"So when I died...." Tahlia did not want to finish the sentence.

235

"You were pregnant, yes." Lucien said sadly. "As soon as the first stone was thrown, the Creator whisked you away. Your child was brought to Eternity in an instant. Neither of you suffered. Your memory was wiped and the Creator allowed the spirit of hope to fill you. You did what you did for your child. In the moment before the first stone hit you, you had done something you'd never done before."

"What was that?" Tahlia asked.

"You prayed." Lucien replied simply. "You asked for forgiveness from the only person who would give it. You begged him to spare your child a violent death. You had no thought of yourself, only the fate of your child."

"Why did he listen after what I'd done?" Tahlia asked in anguish.

"Do you ignore the pleas of your daughters when they are in need? Even when they have done something to displease you?" Lucien asked her.

Tahlia closed her eyes; she didn't know what to say. Her head was pounding and her heart was heavy. No wonder the Creator had not let her remember all these things. No wonder she was spared the truth about her existence before she became the spirit of hope.

"So what now?" Tahlia asked.

"Now, you must accept that you have protected others long enough. The end of an era is near and you have to let go. You will not die, and they do not know about Keira." Lucien told her.

"But if I let go, the spirit of hope will leave me. Keira will be in danger. They will take the opportunity to kill me." Tahlia insisted.

"They won't have the opportunity to kill you. The Creator will not let it happen after everything you have sacrificed in your life. You were not perfect, but you did not let that stop you from fighting for what was right. No one should ever take your child from you without your consent." Lucien told her.

"But that doesn't justify..." Tahlia began.

"No. It doesn't. But the Creator saw past that. He saw in to your heart and knew that you were the vessel he needed. You fought to survive from the very day you were born." Lucien replied.

Tahlia nodded her head, waiting to hear more. She closed her eyes for a moment and all the pain came flooding back. She was tied to a chair again. She was back with the Maladies.

Chapter Twenty-Eight: Nora

"According to this, the Great Hall of the Council of Immortals was in Greece. The Creator lived there too." Hadley told them.

"Yeah, we already knew that from what the Old Immortals told us." Nora replied.

"But, I don't think it was as simple as it being located in Greece. It had to be...inaccessible to mortals." Hadley said.

"How so?" Thatcher asked with interest.

"Look at the similarities between how Dorian describes their home and how mortals described Mount Olympus." Hadley told them.

Thatcher and Nora leaned over to read the passage in the book of Greek Mythology Hadley had placed next to Dorian's notebook. Hadley had read the description of Mount Olympus before, but she hadn't heard Dorian describe Eternity until that evening.

Of course the mythological home of the Greek gods existed in the sky, the grand buildings resting on clouds. In actuality it was a series of ornate buildings carved into the side of a mountain. They were only accessible through a series of tunnels that ran through the interior of the mountain. At the very top stood the Great Hall.

"We're going to Mount Olympus?" Thatcher asked in disbelief.

"Sort of." Hadley replied.

"Do you know where the mountain is? It would be too easy if it was Mount Olympus wouldn't it?" Nora asked.

"Sadly it isn't that simple. In fact, I don't even know that they truly lived in any one place. Eternity covers the entire world. We know that it exists outside of time and space. I think it's more like an empty place that could be anything you need it to be at any given moment." Hadley told them.

"It makes sense that it existed outside of time. A lot of Dorian's journals mention things happening at the same time that we know really happened hundreds of years apart." Thatcher said as he studied one of the journals.

"Wait, do you have the History of the Old Immortals?" Nora asked.

Hadley handed her the book and waited for her to find what she was looking for. Thatcher took a seat next to Hadley and waited patiently.

"Here!" Nora exclaimed. "Lida had the ability to open doors to another plane. It's been under our noses the entire time."

Hadley nodded excitedly but Thatcher seemed to be having trouble processing what Nora had indicated.

"Don't you see? Whitley was trapped in a place that looked like our world but wasn't. Then Keira took Whitley there again at the park. Keira somehow saw into Eternity and opened the door." Nora told them.

"So they're all the same place, they just look different depending on what is happening in that moment?" Thatcher asked slowly. He shook his head as he tried to comprehend what the girls were telling him.

"Look around you! The Creator made all of this. All of the strange and beautiful and vastly different places on Earth. Don't you think he could make another plane that followed different rules than our own?" Nora asked.

There were so many unexplainable pieces of the story the Old Immortals had told them. The discovery of Eternity had gone a long way in explaining many of those pieces, but learning that it could only be accessed by someone with special abilities helped the final pieces fall into place.

"So, let's say for a second that you're not completely crazy and go along with this whole Potteresque 'land of requirement' thing. How exactly would we manage to get there? And how could we guarantee it would get us to the mountain?" Thatcher asked.

Hadley and Nora exchanged a look. The sun would set soon, and they needed to find a place to sleep for a few hours.

"Take us to the ruins of the Mayan temples." Hadley said. "It was the last place they lived before they were cut off completely from the Creator. Maybe we can find evidence of another plane, or an entrance or something."

They packed up the books and took one last look around them before Nora whisked them away.

Chapter Twenty-Nine: Tahlia

The cold water splashed on her face again, forcing her back to consciousness. Her whole body ached and she felt the searing pain of blisters and infected wounds. After she'd awoken from her time in Eternity, the Maladies had left her in a small, windowless room. It was no fun for them to torture her if she couldn't maintain consciousness.

They hadn't fed her for days. She'd been given dirty water to drink that had caused intense intestinal pain. The torture she'd endured previously had been repeated by Pain and Malice many times; the others had left them to continue maiming her.

Despite what Lucien had told her, she tried to hold on. She had to give The Evolved time to accomplish their mission; she had to protect Keira for as long as possible. Now that she had been strapped back into the chair and awoken, she was face to face with the entire group of Maladies once more.

This could only mean one thing; another story time.

"Morning sunshine!" Chaos sang in a less than cordial tone.

"Mmm." Tahlia said as she fought to say something.

"We got tired of you asking so many questions, so Pain decided to put his sewing skills to good use." Malice whispered conspiratorially.

Tahlia was confused at first but the pain she felt when she tried to open her mouth told her everything she needed to know. They had literally sewn her mouth shut.

"Now that we have your undivided attention, let's continue with the lesson shall we?" Avarice said coldly.

Tahlia saw Disease and Vanity off to the sides of the room. Neither had joined in to the torture or storytelling. Vanity was busy brushing her hair, and Disease was attempting to apply ointment to his pustules. She rolled her eyes, she may not be allowed to speak, but she was definitely going to give them attitude.

"The worst part about being trapped in that sphere was that the Creator had somehow figured out what Absalom was up to and decided to stuff one more thing into our already close quarters. Elpis. Hope. You." Avarice said in a voice that dripped with disdain.

Tahlia didn't know how they remembered being in the sphere. Her earliest memory was speaking to Pandora after being released. She was now thankful that the Creator had spared her any earlier memories.

"By the time that woman finally listened to Absalom, we were ready to get away from all the light and warmth you brought with you. We took off as fast as we could so we wouldn't have to bear another minute with you." Rage told her.

"By then of course Absalom had been found out and banished. We helped him get out of the underworld just as he had released us.

He soon became our leader and we served him happily for many years. We helped kill many of the worthless descendants of the Council of Immortals. But, he kept us on a tight leash." Chaos said.

"Now that he's gone, we can do whatever we want. The bits of evil he had left all over the world allowed us to directly infect people instead of having to worm our way in. The only thing standing between us and the perfect world we envisioned is you." Malice said simply as she drove a knife deep into Tahlia's gut.

"Mmmmm!" The scream threatened to pull her lips apart.

She felt the knife slide out of her then slowly slide back in at another location. The pain was intense. She started to black out again but was forced back to consciousness by a needle poke straight to the heart.

"This adrenaline stuff can be deadly in high doses. I wonder what it will feel like if you can't die." Pain said as he tossed the syringe away.

Her heart was pounding, her whole body felt like it was vibrating. She just wanted the pain to stop as Malice slammed a knife into each thigh. Her cold laughter filled the room around her. Tahlia had lost so much blood and endured so much torture that she didn't know how much more she could take.

Malice seemed to want to test just that as she gripped each knife firmly and slowly dragged them through her legs. The agony of knives ripping through muscles and tendons as they scraped bone and slowly came to a stop left Tahlia retching from the pain.

The vomit oozed between the stiches that had been cruelly sewn into her lips but the majority of it went back down her throat. The burn of acid and bile caused Tahlia to heave once more. The force of her heave caused her to rip the stitches on her lips.

A mixture of vomit and blood poured from her mouth as the Maladies looked on. Tahlia could take it no more.

"Please!" She cried out. "Please end this."

"If only it were that simple." Rage said. "Keep going."

Tahlia closed her eyes and let the tears slide down her face. She remembered what Lucien had told her. She had to let go. It was time for her to surrender and allow the spirit to find a new vessel. She didn't know how she was supposed to do that. Her heart sank as she thought about spending the rest of her life in this endless torture. She would never see her family again. She would never have the chance to share her story with her daughters. She would never be with Eric.

It was hopeless.

In that moment, a blinding light flew from Tahlia's chest and hit the Maladies in full force. They fell to the ground unmoving. The light hovered before Tahlia for a few moments before swirling around her in a motion that resembled an embrace. When it had finished, the light flew away through the hole in the ceiling.

Instantly, the pain was gone. This must be death. Tahlia waited patiently for the darkness to claim her, but instead she heard a voice.

"Tahlia, you are free. You are whole and you are free. You have served me faithfully. I am only sorry I could not prevent what you have endured here." The Creator told her.

Tahlia felt her face, she felt her legs and then she felt her stomach. The wounds were all gone. He had healed her. She stood and stumbled forward.

"You must go now. Call out for Nora while they sleep." The Creator told her.

Tahlia nodded and stumbled outside without glancing back.

"Nora!" She called into the darkness of the night. "Nora!"

"Tahlia?" Nora asked.

It was so dark that Tahlia couldn't see anything around her. There was no moon in the sky and no lights nearby. She tentatively took a step forward, hearing the crunch of gravel beneath her feet.

"Nora, where are you?" Tahlia whispered.

A hand touched her shoulder; she jumped and a small scream escaped her. The hand grasped her tighter and she felt a pull near her navel. Soon the darkness gave way to light as they appeared in the library at their home.

"Tahlia! What happened to you?" Dorian said with fear in his voice.

Tahlia looked down at her clothes. Her shirt was ripped and covered in blood and vomit. Her jeans had two slices straight down her thighs. There wasn't an inch of her body that didn't appear to be covered in blood and vomit.

"I..." Tahlia didn't know how to explain what happened to her and didn't know if she wanted to. She bit her lip and put her head down as the tears ran down her face.

"It's alright." Nora said softly. "Let's get you cleaned up."

"Let me do it. Go back to Hadley and Thatcher. Let them know she's home." Whitley told her.

Nora nodded and disappeared.

Whitley approached her and Tahlia fell into her daughter's arms sobbing. She had let herself to believe she would never see her daughters again. She allowed herself to be led to her room.

"I'm going to go start the shower." Whitley told her.

A thought of water cascading over her in endless torrents flashed into her mind.

"No. I would rather take a bath." Tahlia said softly.

"Alright then. I'll run a bath." Whitley replied.

When Whitley came back out of the bathroom she excused herself to go change. Her clothes had been covered in the same substances Tahlia's bore when she had accepted a hug from her mother. Tahlia made her way to the bathroom and began to undress. Her body showed no signs of the injuries she had sustained.

She threw the clothes in the trash and stepped into the tub. The water was the perfect temperature. As she sank in to the water she quickly grabbed the soap and began to scrub her body clean. The water around her slowly turned pink from the blood that had been caked all over her.

Draining the water from the tub, she decided to go ahead and turn the shower on. She quickly washed her hair and turned off the water. Once her hair was wrapped in a towel, she wrapped another around her body and stood before the mirror. She leaned forward to take a closer look at her lips where she had torn through the stitching. There were no scars, it was as though none of it had ever happened; but the memories remained.

"Mom?" Whitley had reappeared.

Tahlia turned to her daughter and tried to smile. Whitley pulled a face and indicated that she should brush her teeth. When Tahlia turned back to the mirror she saw the blood that appeared to have dried on her teeth. She quickly brushed them and used some mouthwash.

When she made her way back into her bedroom, she put on the sweatpants and tank top Whitley had laid out for her.

"I need to go talk to everyone. You all need to know what happened and what I learned." Tahlia told her quietly.

They made their way downstairs and found everyone waiting for them in the library. Nora had brought Hadley and Thatcher back with her and had also found Eric. He stood and strode straight to her. She allowed him to pull her into his arms and kiss her gently. She wondered how he would react to the story she was about to tell.

Chapter Thirty: Keira

She opened her eyes in the dim light of her room. She looked at the table next to the bed and was surprised to find the small lamp was not on. As she began to wonder where the light was coming from, she saw it.

There was a light hovering at the foot of her bed. It seemed to be more than just a light as small wisps appeared to flow from it as it floated. There was something about this light that called to her. She wasn't afraid.

Keira stood on her bed and walked to the light. It smelled of spring and sunlight and cast no shadows in her room despite the bright contrast to the rest of the room. Keira reached forward and touched the glowing orb.

As soon as she made contact with the light it began to change. It circled her and wound its way around her like a cat rubbing against its owner. She giggled at the sensation.

The light began to flow into her as though it were claiming her for its own. She opened her arms and invited it in. Her heart felt light and whole. This was what it was to be the vessel. This was what it was to be hope.

When the last of the light was absorbed by her body, she floated up slightly then fell lightly to the bed and was soon fast asleep.

When she woke, she got out of bed and bounded down the stairs in search of her family. She had to find out what happened to Tahlia. She knew that if she had become the vessel, something terrible had happened.

She came sliding into the kitchen to find everyone gathered around the table drinking coffee. Her eyes met Tahlia's and she squealed in delight when she saw that she was alright. Keira ran for her and flung her arms around Tahlia's neck.

"Lia! I'm so glad you're alright." Keira whispered in her ear. "After the light came to me I thought it meant you were gone."

Tahlia pulled away for a moment and looked at her. A slight look of concern crossed over her face as she examined Keira.

"The light?" Tahlia asked.

"Yes. It was above my bed. It went in here." She said proudly pointing to her chest.

Everyone at the table looked at each other as though accepting the fact that Keira had welcomed the spirit of hope into herself.

Keira smiled at her parents and grandfathers. She knew her mom, Hadley and Thatcher would be leaving again soon. Keira climbed down from Tahlia's lap and went to kiss her mother. As soon as she planted the kiss on Nora's cheek, Nora began to glow.

Chapter Thirty-One: Kerr

Keira gasped and stepped back from Nora. White light shot from Nora's hands and she floated up from her chair. Kerr watched as his wife's head relax back and a serene smile spread across her face. It was beautiful.

When she came back down to the ground she opened her eyes and smiled. Thatcher and Hadley cheered and Kerr let out a whoop. Keira seemed confused for a moment until her mother swooped her up in her arms and covered her in kisses.

"The beginning will come from within me." Nora mused as she looked at her daughter, then gave Kerr a small smile.

"Geez, now Kerr is the only one left. You always were a bit slow." Thatcher joked as he nudged his friend.

He laughed at Thatcher's joke, but couldn't help but feel a twinge of frustration. Kerr knew his time would come, his prophecy still rang in his head every day, he was supposed to embrace the present. He tried his best to do that every day, but his visions and concerns about the future were often at the forefront of his mind. He wasn't sure how or when his prophecy would be fulfilled, but he knew it would be when he had truly accepted the present for what it was.

Later, after Nora and the other Evolved had left, Keira convinced Dorian and Romulus to play outside with her. They set to work building a fort for her to play in. They used blankets and clothespins to create the enclosure between two bushes next to the patio.

Kerr watched them from the kitchen window as he washed the dishes from breakfast. He loved to see Dorian and Romulus play with their granddaughter.

When they had finished, Keira ran in to get Kerr so he could play with her. Kerr came out and stood smiling at the fort appreciatively.

"Wow, this is a great fort sweet pea!" Kerr told her.

"Papa and Grampa helped me." She replied with a hint of pride in her voice.

Kerr laughed at her and followed her in to the fort. When his eyes adjusted he realized something was off. They weren't inside a fort in the backyard. They were in a cave.

"Keira?" Kerr asked uncertainly.

"Can you believe it? I can do magic. I was picturing my fort as a cave, and it became one." Keira said proudly.

Kerr didn't respond right away. He was concerned about where they had ended up. Was Keira developing the same abilities as her mother? Had she transported them somewhere?

"Where are we little one?" Kerr asked her.

"I don't know, Lida told me I could open a door whenever I wanted. So I did." Keira told him.

"I see. So, where did the door lead us? Into a cave?" Kerr asked her.

"I don't know. But let's look outside!" Keira said excitedly.

Kerr followed her to the mouth of the cave. He couldn't believe his eyes. They were up high, and from the dying light around them, he registered that they hadn't truly been in a cave at all. He looked down to see steep stone stairs leading to an open grassy area. There were other buildings in ruin around them. He knew this place.

He took Keira's hand and held on tight. Somehow, the little girl had brought them to Mutul. He had seen this place in Romulus' memory. The ancient city had once been teeming with life. This was where the natives had offered their virgin daughters as sacrifices to the Old Immortals; mistaking them for gods. This was where the future of the Old Immortals had been irrevocably altered. Did Keira feel a connection with this place because of her roots? Her namesake had been born here;

Romulus' wife had given birth to Keiran in this very structure.

"How did we get here Keira?" Kerr asked her cautiously. "Do you know what made you bring us here?"

"No. I was just thinking about a cave, but this is so much better right?" Keira said excitedly.

A ball of light appeared from the trees. It floated across the open courtyard below, illuminating the ruins of the village below. Kerr picked Keira up and carefully stepped back into the opening behind them. He motioned for Keira to be quiet.

Suddenly, three people appeared before them in the shadows. Kerr held on to Keira, ready to defend his daughter if the new visitors posed a threat.

"Turn the light back on! I can't see a thing." A girl whispered.

Kerr would know that voice anywhere. He set Keira down before the ball of light reappeared in front of them. He found himself face to face with Hadley, Nora and Thatcher.

Chapter Thirty-Two: Nora

"Keira!" Nora yelled in surprise. "What are you doing here young lady? Kerr! What were you thinking?"

"Mommy, I built a fort with Papa and Grampa and turned it into a cave!" Keira said excitedly. "But, how did you get here?"

Nora looked at Kerr, hoping for an explanation. Kerr looked just as lost as she was.

"She took me into her fort and said she decided to think of it as a cave. As soon as she did, we appeared inside here. When I came out, I realized we were not in a cave at all." Kerr told her.

"No. You're in Guatemala, with our daughter." Nora said with a hint of frustration.

"This is where the Old Immortals lived. This is Mutul." Kerr told them. "Nora,

Thatcher, some of our mortal ancestors are from here."

"That's great." Nora said sounding utterly unenthused.

She took a deep breath in the humid air. She needed to get Keira and Kerr home.

"Alright you two, I don't know how you got here, but I'm going to take you home." Nora told them.

"Mommy, you're never going to get through there without me." Keira said pointing back at the opening of the temple they stood on.

Nora dropped to her knees in front of her daughter. She felt the temperature drop to a more acceptable level. Nora was thankful to have Hadley along. Nora and Thatcher had done their parts by shielding them and providing light respectively.

"What do you mean baby?" Nora asked her daughter.

"You need me to open the door remember?" Keira told her.

Nora didn't know what to say to that. She looked at her daughter then back at Kerr.

"Open the door to what honey?" Kerr asked.

"Duh! To Eternity." Keira told them.

Hadley was dancing back and forth on her tip toes trying to get Nora's attention.

"Yes Hadley?" Nora asked her patiently.

"This is a door to Eternity. This location will take us directly to the mountain!" Hadley told her excitedly.

"Yes mommy!" Keira squealed pulling on her mother's shirt.

Nora looked down at her daughter, unsure how or why she would know anything about opening a portal to another plane. She smiled at Keira and pulled her in for a hug.

"What made you decide to come here now?" Nora asked her.

"I felt like you needed me." Keira told her.

"Alright, I'll let you open the door, but then you have to go home." Nora said.

"Sorry mommy, that's not how it works. I have to go with you. So does daddy." Keira said putting her foot down.

Nora was taken aback by the firm response she received from her daughter. She wondered how her daughter could be so certain, but decided that she had to have faith that her amazingly powerful little girl knew what she was talking about. Nora looked around at the other Evolved, they all seemed to have come to the same conclusion she had.

"Alright honey, what do we do next?" Nora asked her.

Keira smiled and took her mother's hand, signaling for the others to follow her.

Chapter Thirty-Three: Thatcher

One moment they were heading into the darkness of the temple opening, the next they were standing at the foot of a mountain.

Thatcher looked up at the enormous mountain in front of him. It was so tall he couldn't see the top. The place seemed to be long abandoned and empty yet everything was in perfect condition. The foot of the mountain boasted a large cave mouth that appeared to be the only entrance.

As his eyes traveled higher he saw structures jutting out from various levels. The structures mainly mimicked Greek architecture but there were hints of other traditions along the way. The clouds appeared to be covering the top of the mountain, hiding the Great Hall from view.

"Holy crap." Hadley said into the stunned silence.

Thatcher smiled at her warmly. She was staring open-mouthed at the mountain before them. He looked at Kerr, then at Nora still grasping Keira's hand. They had arrived.

"So, now what?" Thatcher asked.

"We go inside." Kerr said with a shrug.

"We explore." Hadley said.

"We see the Creator and get some answers." Nora finished.

Keira took off running toward the mountain.

"What are you waiting for? Can't you hear it?" Keira called over her shoulder as her dark curls bounced around her face.

Thatcher exchanged a confused look with the other Evolved. He hadn't heard anything. He strained his ears for a moment, waiting for the hint of a sound when it hit him.

"It's laughter." Thatcher said in awe. It was more than just laughter it was laughter that called to his soul. It felt like coming home.

The others seemed to pick up on it too and they began to follow Keira with excitement. When they arrived at the foot of the mountain they didn't hesitate as they stepped into the yawning darkness. As soon as they stepped through they found themselves in a sparkling room filled with light.

Thatcher tried to take it all in, the tiny balls of multi-colored light were floating everywhere; the twinkle of each little orb gave the room a prismatic quality. It was breathtakingly beautiful. The large entry filled him with an elation he had never experienced.

"What is this?" Thatcher asked.

Nora turned to him, tears running down her face. "These are the souls that haven't gotten to live in our world. Some are yet to be born, others were lost or taken before they took their first breath."

"How do you know?" He whispered in awe.

"Call it mothers' intuition, but I feel them. My heart breaks for the lost potential but I can't help but feel the hope and happiness that they will be given another chance. They're all so beautiful." Nora told him.

"Wow." Thatcher couldn't think of anything to sum up his feelings.

Keira came running over to them to tell them they had to go up the stairs. Kerr and Nora followed her but as Thatcher began to fall in step behind them he saw Hadley staring at the lights unmoving. He went to her, unsure of how she was feeling.

"Hadley, it's time to go upstairs." Thatcher said gently.

"Thatcher! Look! This one is ours." Hadley whispered excitedly.

"What?" He was surprised by her words.

"I feel it. I could hear this little one calling to me." She pointed directly at a twinkling green light.

"Hi there little guy." The light grew slightly brighter at Thatcher's words. As the light brightened, another emerged from behind it.

"Amazing." Kerr said behind them.

Thatcher turned and grinned at his friend. "Apparently we're having two babies. These two." He pointed.

"Yeah well, you'll have to ask me a certain question first won't you?" Hadley teased as she slowly turned to head for the stairs where Nora and Keira waited for them.

Thatcher cleared his throat and got down on one knee. Hadley turned around and her jaw dropped. Thatcher had been carrying the ring around with him for nearly a year, waiting for the right moment.

"What are you doing?" Hadley asked.

"Hadley, I have been in love with you for what feels like a lifetime. You are an amazing, intelligent, beautiful woman and I don't deserve you, but for some reason you've chosen me." Thatcher paused and pulled the ring out of his jacket pocket.

Hadley was crying tears of joy, quietly waiting for him to continue.

"I want to spend eternity loving you, what better place to ask you to be my wife than in Eternity?" Thatcher asked

"Hadley Anne Callaghan, will you marry me?" Thatcher asked.

She nodded her head and held out her hand. The ring slid onto her finger and she giggled as she threw her arms around his neck. He kissed his fiancé and held her for a few moments as she stared into his eyes.

Nora and Kerr approached them and offered their congratulations. Keira ran over to see what the fuss was about. Thatcher felt as though his heart could burst with happiness; he was surrounded by his family and Hadley was going to marry him.

They made their way up the stairs, each step bringing them closer to the laughter they had heard before they entered. It wasn't constant, the sound reminded Thatcher of a distant party. They came to a landing after climbing for what could have been hours or seconds.

The landing was circular and had doors lining the curved wall. Thatcher approached one of the doors and pushed it open. Inside he found what appeared to be a bedroom. The room looked as though it had been deserted long ago. He noticed a golden statue sitting on a table near the open-air windows. Thatcher had seen the statue before; it was a woman, blindfolded and holding her scales high.

"Thatcher?" Kerr called to him from the door.

"I'm in here. Look at this." Thatcher said pointing to the statue.

"You shouldn't be in here." Kerr told him carefully.

"Why? It doesn't look like anyone has been in here in years." Thatcher told him.

"Exactly. This was Absalom's room." Kerr replied.

Thatcher looked around him once more. His eyes took in the room that had once housed a mass murderer. He didn't see anything that would have indicated what Absalom would become. He felt a shiver run through him as he glanced back at the statue of Themis, Goddess of Justice. How could someone who admired something as noble as justice have become such a monster? He couldn't help but think about what he'd read in the History of Old Immortals all those years ago. If Absalom had been rotten from the beginning, why did he care about justice?

"I don't get it." Thatcher mused aloud.

"Hmm?" Kerr made a questioning sound.

"What made him change?" Thatcher asked. "I mean, this statue stands for justice, for a balance between right and wrong. But he went completely off the rails."

Kerr looked at him for a moment as though deciding what to say. "The thing about justice is, it is never fair in the eyes of all those affected by its touch. When justice is brought to a killer, the family of the victim may feel relief, but those who believed the killer was innocent would view the ruling as unfair."

Thatcher thought about that for a moment. "For Absalom, justice wasn't about right and wrong it was about balance. Maybe he was unhappy with the love the Creator felt for man just as the Maladies were upset by the love the Creator felt for the Council of Immortals. He wanted to ruin the perfect creation of man by corrupting and harming them. Absalom thought that he was correcting the balance of power by destroying the descendants of the Old Immortals. In his mind, he was delivering justice. What a twisted freak."

Kerr nodded emphatically and gestured for Thatcher to follow him.

Thatcher began to follow Kerr but stopped and gave the room one more look. There was something final about standing in this place, something that left him feeling at peace.

"I forgive him. I can't really explain it, but I'm not going to be angry anymore. He killed his own son trying to do what he thought was right. I don't agree with what he did, but I have to forgive him." Thatcher said with finality.

"Yeah you do." Hadley's voice came from behind him.

She opened her arms and he went into them willingly. Thatcher knew she'd been waiting for him to let go of the rest of the anger he had been clinging to. Standing in this room, he finally found the strength he needed to let go and move on.

"Let's go. They're waiting for us in the hallway. Let's go see if we can find out where that laughter is coming from." Hadley said before she planted a quick kiss on his cheek.

Making their way up the next flight of stairs they realized they would reach the source of the laughter when they made it to the top. It was strange because Kerr described the laughter as a man's voice, Nora described it much the same as Thatcher heard it, as both a man and a woman. Hadley and Keira could hear a whole room of people. None of them could explain the differences in what they heard.

Finally, they saw a bright white light at the top of the stairs ahead of them. As they reached the top, they came face to face with a room full of people they had been aching to see.

"Thatcher!" His mother rushed forward to pull him into a tight embrace.

He was so shocked to be in his mother's arms that he pulled away to look at her face. When he did, he saw the joy etched on every inch. Glancing up, he saw his father standing proudly behind her.

"Dad? Mom?" Thatcher asked uncertainly.

"It's us Firecracker." His father said, bringing back the memory of his childhood nickname.

"I've missed you so much." He said, then realizing he needed to say more he told them what was on his heart. "I'm so sorry I couldn't stop the fire."

"We know it wasn't you son. You were so young. We've missed you too." His mother said with a serene smile.

A small cry escaped Hadley as Thatcher was crushed into a strong hug with his parents. That small cry was all it took for him, he began grieving lost time and rejoicing in the reunion through his tears.

GROWING hope

Chapter Thirty-Four: Kerr

The room held more people than he could count. He scanned the room and realized it was set up to be comfortable and functional. There were couches placed around the room and everyone appeared to be having wonderful conversations.

He felt his father before he saw him. Kerr strode into the crowd, leaving Thatcher in the arms of his parents. A group of men were gathered around his father, they all held the same features as Kerr himself.

"Kerr!" Cole Mason exclaimed.

He stood staring at the man he had seen burst into flames all those years before. He choked back tears as his father closed the gap between them and pulled him into a strong embrace.

"It's so good to see you son." Cole said into his son's neck.

"You too dad. I never would have imagined I'd see you again." Kerr told him.

Cole nodded his agreement. He glanced over Kerr's shoulder, his eyes growing wide. Kerr turned to see what had caught his father's attention. Nora was holding Keira and approaching them with a small smile on her face.

"Dad, this is Nora. She's my wife. And this, is our daughter, Keira." Kerr told his father proudly.

"I know son. But it's still wonderful to meet you both. I'm a grandpa!" He laughed and reached for Keira.

Kerr smiled widely as his daughter hugged his father. He was witnessing a moment he never thought he would see. Nora took his hand as they were approached by a man who bore a striking resemblance to Kerr.

"I am Keiran." The young man said.

"Oh, wow." Nora said breathlessly.

"I am honored to meet you both." Keiran told them both.

"It's nice to meet you too." Kerr replied, still reeling from the idea of standing in front of Romulus' son.

"We would like for you to meet Keira, we named her after you." Nora told him with a grin.

Keira smiled shyly at her many times great-grandfather and gave him a small wave. Kerr heard Nora inhale sharply beside him and felt her grab his arm. He looked up in time to see a woman who looked remarkably like his wife walking toward them.

The woman came up to them, smiling through the tears in her eyes. She laughed out loud like the joy was bursting from her body as she stopped in front of Nora.

"Hello Nora." She said carefully.

"Hi mom." Nora said in a state of shock.

"You've grown into such a beautiful young woman." Her mother said as she reached up to touch her daughter's face. Nora leaned her head into her mother's hand and closed her eyes.

"I wish I could remember you." Nora told her mother apologetically.

"Oh baby, you were so young. How could you have remembered me? You were only an infant. I only wish we'd had more time together." She said sadly.

Kerr didn't want to interrupt this special moment but he wanted to make sure Nora's mom met her granddaughter. He cleared his throat and reached out a hand to introduce himself.

"I'm Kerr. I have the honor of being married to your daughter." He said proudly.

"Of course. I'm Elizabeth Lowell. It's wonderful to meet you. And little Keira too." Elizabeth said with a smile.

A man approached them from behind Elizabeth and introduced himself as Nora's father, Donovan. Nora hugged both of her parents but still seemed to be shocked by the whole situation.

Kerr soon found that the room was full of those who had been murdered by Absalom in his quest to destroy the Evolved. They met descendants of the rest of the council and shared a warm and friendly conversation with Thatcher and his parents. He remembered that Nora and Thatcher's mothers were sisters when he saw them together and knew the resemblances couldn't be denied.

"Nora, this is your aunt, Sophia." Elizabeth told her.

Sophia nodded at Nora and introduced her to Thatcher's father, Ross. Kerr was pleased to see that Sophia had immediately latched on to Hadley as they stood with the rest of the Evolved.

They found their way to some couches and spent what could have been days sharing stories and reminiscing about the times they had actually shared with their families. Of course it occurred to Kerr that they had all been able to keep tabs on them while here in Eternity, but the idea that they had all been just outside of reach every time he had a vision was almost too much for him to comprehend.

Keira had fallen asleep in his lap. He shifted her weight slightly and her curls fell across her round face. Kerr noticed Cole, Elizabeth and Donovan watching her as she slept. He couldn't imagine how they were feeling as they talked to the children they'd been forced to leave behind. And it must have been even more difficult to spend time with the grandchild they would have to watch grow from afar.

A quiet crept over the room and the people around them slowly seemed to fade away until the only people left were the Evolved and their parents.

"It is time for you to continue on your journey. You still have another stop to make before you will arrive at the Great Hall." Cole told them.

As each of them said their goodbyes, they watched their departed family members slowly fade until they were left standing in an empty room.

"Come on guys, let's get going." Hadley said.

Kerr could feel the strain in her voice. She was the only one who hadn't faced a long-departed relative. He could imagine how concerned she was over the possible reactions they may have. But as far as Kerr could see, the meeting with their parents had left Thatcher, Nora and himself feeling rejuvenated for the journey ahead.

Chapter Thirty-Five: Dorian

It had been weeks since Tahlia had returned. The disappearance of Kerr and Keira had concerned him for a moment, but Romulus assured him that nothing had happened. The Evolved must have called on them so Keira could open the door to Eternity. He spent his days helping Tahlia cope with what had happened to her while she was held by the Maladies.

She had finally shared everything about her experiences with both Dorian and Romulus a few nights after she returned. She was still coming to terms with the fact that she had allowed herself to give up despite sharing the details of her conversation with Lucien. She blamed herself for the danger Keira would face when the Maladies discovered that she was no longer the threat they needed to destroy.

Dorian sat staring intently at the fireplace. The warmth coming from the fire that burned within it allowed him to momentarily forget the howling winds of early October outside. One thing he could count on about South Dakota was the lack of a lengthy transition from fall to winter; the leaves fell and immediately brought on the bitter cold.

Romulus entered the library and sat down on the large chair opposite Dorian. He didn't need to speak for Dorian to understand what he was thinking. They had both been worried about the Evolved and their granddaughter through the transition of the spirit of hope. They had never encountered the spirit entering a new vessel and didn't know what to expect. The Maladies had been surprisingly quiet since they'd been knocked on their butts by the Creator and the spirit of hope. They weren't sure if that should be a relief or a sign of things that would be coming.

"Have you spoken with Tahlia this evening?" Romulus asked in a quiet voice.

"No. I haven't spoken to her since this morning when we talked about the torture she'd endured." Dorian told him.

"I saw her a few moments ago. She was in the kitchen staring out the back window. I fear she is in a fragile state." Romulus shared.

"I think you're right. But only time can heal the emotional wounds she has had inflicted upon her. It's a good sign that she's willing to talk about it." Dorian replied.

"Does it bother you at all that she lost hope?" Romulus asked.

"That depends on what you mean. It bothers me that she found herself in a position that led her to feel like she would never see her family again. It bothers me that she was tortured and taunted for weeks. But if you're asking if it bothers me that she let the go of the spirit of hope, the answer is no." Dorian told him thoughtfully.

"Can you elaborate?" Romulus asked, his voice brimming with curiosity.

"I believe that if she had not let go, she would still be there. They would still be torturing her. We would still be desperately searching for her. I believe that the Creator recognized that moment as the one in which she had fulfilled her obligations as the vessel. He told her she had served him faithfully, and I believe he was right." Dorian paused for a moment. "Tahlia is a strong woman and has been the sole source of hope in seemingly hopeless times. She had given up a lot to be that light for the world."

Romulus nodded his head in agreement. Dorian knew his brother saw all the same qualities in Tahlia as he did himself, but sometimes it felt good to hear your thoughts verified by another. Romulus' concern for Tahlia came from a place of love while Dorian's belief that everything happened as it should came from a place of faith.

"Now that Nora has fulfilled her prophecy, I am no longer immortal." Dorian told his brother carefully.

"How can you tell?" Romulus asked curiously.

"I can feel it in my body. The power is no longer there. I feel like I am in perfect health, but my energy and strength come from my physical body now rather than from a deeper place." Dorian said simply.

"I wonder how old you are physically." Romulus mused.

Dorian laughed aloud at that thought. He hadn't really considered it before, but he truly didn't know how old his body was. He had never had to wonder about lifespan or physical health because he had always had the advantage of immortality.

"Well, I suppose I'd better visit a doctor." Dorian replied with a smile.

The door to the library opened as the two brothers shared a laugh. Dorian looked up to see Tahlia enter the room. She joined him on the couch and pulled a blanket over her lap.

"What's so funny?" Tahlia asked.

"Dorian's going to get a physical." Romulus replied as he shook with controlled laughter.

Tahlia grinned at the men she had known her whole life. She shook her head as she joined in the laughter. Dorian knew that no matter what happened, they would always have each other and that meant more to him than anything in the world.

"Alright boys, I have some serious stuff to discuss with you." Tahlia told them, bringing an end to their fits of giggles.

"You have the floor." Dorian replied.

"Eric has asked me to marry him. Again." Tahlia said with a smile.

"That's wonderful news!" Romulus said excitedly.

"Have you said yes?" Dorian asked her.

"I didn't at first. At first I told him I couldn't. But then I realized that I have the rest of my life ahead of me. I'm not dead. I'm not going to die yet. I may not be much help these days, but I am certainly not going to let the Maladies stop me from moving on with my life. The Creator has given me a second chance and I won't waste it." Tahlia replied firmly.

"You seem as though you feel guilty about this." Romulus said carefully.

"I do. My whole life I've put myself last because it was my duty to make sure everyone else had the will to carry on through all their trials and tribulations. And learning about what I did and who I was before becoming the vessel makes me wonder why I even deserve this. It's not easy to reframe my perspective around just being a normal person." Tahlia shared quietly.

"Well, let me ease your mind on one thing." Dorian paused with a sparkle in his eyes. "You will never be a normal person."

293

He couldn't contain it any longer and allowed himself to giggle again. It felt wonderful to have his brother and sister join with him in childish laughter. They were entering a new season in their lives and would soon be growing old together. He couldn't think of any other people he would want to have by his side as his life entered the next phase.

Chapter Thirty-Six: Thatcher

They had continued up the stairs and journeyed for an undeterminable amount of time. When they came to the next landing they found themselves in a room that looked like it belonged in their world rather than in Eternity.

The room was set up like a studio apartment. A couch and television were sitting off to the left in the corner of the room. A bed sat in the corner opposite. There were bookshelves filled with many titles that Thatcher himself had read at least once.

"Wonder who lives here." Hadley said as she scanned the room.

"Not a clue. Look, there's another staircase. Let's go." Nora said heading across the room.

"Leaving so soon?" Asked a voice from their right.

Thatcher turned to see the owner of the voice emerging from what appeared to be a bathroom. He couldn't' believe what he was seeing.

Malcolm stood before them looking whole and healthy. He held his hands out and spun around to show them he was really there.

"I know, I look different since you last saw me. I've gained some weight. Right here." He said pointing at the spot where Absalom had blown a hole in his chest.

"It's so good to see you." Thatcher said, his voice catching in his throat.

The last time he had been with Malcolm, the young boy had died to save him. He had viewed him as a younger brother and had been so heartbroken when Malcolm had given his life for him.

"Well, I'd say the same, but I've been able to see you guys the whole time. Congratulations on the babies by the way.

If only I could pull a Lazarus like Whitley." Malcolm winked.

"Malcolm, do you know how much farther it is to the Great Hall?" Kerr asked him.

"Nice to see you too Kerr." Malcolm joked. "It's actually the next level."

"Wow, I see how you rate." Thatcher told him with a laugh.

"I'm not the only one who lives on this level. I'm just the only one you guys get to see. This is the level reserved for those of us who sacrifice ourselves for the world." Malcolm said.

"So do you have Jesus over to play video games?" Thatcher asked him.

"Yeah actually. He's pretty good at Smash Brothers." Malcolm replied with a grin.

They all laughed but Thatcher couldn't help but be left speechless at the thought of playing video games with Jesus.

"Have a seat. I'm supposed to make sure you guys get rested up and take a shower." Malcolm said.

"I'd rather just finish the next flight of stairs. Keira is getting heavy." Kerr told Malcolm kindly.

"No can do. The problem is, you guys are running on different physical time than those of us here in Eternity. See according to traditional time, you've been climbing stairs for about a month. You haven't used the bathroom, you haven't slept and you haven't eaten in 28 days." Malcolm said.

Thatcher was surprised by this thought. Time and space didn't matter in Eternity. Why would they have to even consider traditional time during their journey there?

"I can see the wheels turning in those heads. Here's the thing. You guys are adults. Keira is a child. Haven't you noticed that she's getting tired? Your bodies won't tire as quickly as hers but you do need to rest up before you continue. You all need to eat and rest. As soon as you leave here, you'll meet with the Creator and then be thrust back into battle." Malcolm explained.

"Battle?" Hadley asked with concern.

"Well yeah, do you think the Maladies have just given up? They might be licking their wounds from the aftermath of messing with Tahlia, but they're getting ready to strike again." Malcolm said.

"Then what are we waiting for?" Nora demanded.

"I know you want to make sure your daughter is protected but you can't go running into battle without having slept for a month." Malcolm reiterated.

"I feel fine." Nora replied irritably.

"Yeah, now. But what about when you leave Eternity? That's when your lack of attention to your physical body will hit you." Malcolm retorted.

Thatcher understood what Malcolm was telling them but also understood the urgency in Nora's plea. If they were here and the Maladies attacked, the Old Immortals would be defenseless.

"Okay, we'll eat and rest and shower. Then we're moving on." Thatcher said sternly.

Malcolm smiled and clapped his hands. As soon as he clapped the room transformed into a dining room. The table before them was laid out with every possible food they could want. Pizza, pasta, salad, fruits and vegetables were lined up right alongside a large roast and some roasted chicken. Thatcher felt his stomach rumble and his mouth started to water.

"Yummy! Mommy, I'm hungry." Keira said rousing from her slumber in Kerr's arms.

They laughed in response and settled in to eat. Their dinner conversation was relaxed and familial as they chatted about life and Eternity. Malcolm seemed to have adjusted nicely despite dying so young.

Kerr, Nora and Keira excused themselves to use Malcolm's bathroom. They emerged about an hour later looking clean and refreshed. Hadley took her turn next while the Mason's excused themselves to sleep. Malcolm had made a bedroom available for each of them.

"So, you're engaged." Malcolm asked.

Thatcher smiled widely, but wasn't sure where this conversation was going. "Yes, and apparently we're going to have kids."

"They'll both be boys. A couple more just like you." Malcolm told him with a grin.

"What's wrong with that?" Thatcher asked with a laugh.

"Oh, nothing! I just think it will be interesting." Malcolm said.

"You have no idea. I'm excited to marry her, and I'm glad Hadley and I are going to work through everything that happened..." Thatcher replied.

"But...." Malcolm prodded.

"But I'm afraid of what would happen if the Maladies infected me again?" Thatcher asked desperately.

"There it is." Malcolm said.

"There it is." Thatcher replied.

"Here's the deal, you aren't going to get infected again." Malcolm said matter-of-factly.

"Oh yeah? When did you get so wise?" Thatcher asked.

"I'm not wise. I'm just telling you that you can't live like that. You can't constantly live in a state of 'what-if'. You have to live with the thought that everything will work out for the best and if it doesn't you deal with it then." Malcolm told him.

Thatcher thought for a moment. He knew Malcolm was right. But the fear was still there, a fear he wasn't sure he could overcome.

"Why did you do it?" Thatcher asked him suddenly.

"Because I needed to. I knew that if you died, Absalom would live and grow more powerful. I knew that if I lived, Absalom would destroy the rest of the Evolved and make me watch, then he would make me kill the other Old Immortals. The world would have become his playhouse." Malcolm said with a shudder.

"But how did you know those things?" Thatcher asked.

"I really can't explain it. It happened in a few seconds. I saw what he was going to do, and knew what it would mean. I had to stop him. I was never supposed to be one of the Evolved. It had to be me or it wouldn't work." Malcolm replied.

Thatcher thought for a moment and realized that Malcolm had done more than die for him, he had died for the good of mankind. Even if he wasn't one of the Evolved, he was still an important player in the fate of the world. If Malcolm hadn't died that day, the world would have suffered. The Creators plans wouldn't have come to pass. Thatcher looked up to see Hadley come out of the bathroom wrapped in a towel. She grinned sheepishly and made her way into the bedroom Malcolm had assigned to her.

"I better go shower." Thatcher said.

"About time. You wreak." Malcolm laughed.

Thatcher shoved Malcolm playfully and made his way to the bathroom.

Chapter Thirty-Seven: Whitley

She woke in the darkness wrapped in blankets. She heard voices outside her room. The urgency with which they spoke led her to detangle herself quickly and throw open her bedroom door.

Whitley made her way down the hall to the top of the stairs. She sat down quickly when she saw Tahlia, Dorian and Romulus standing in the large entry. The only light that shone down on them came from moon pouring through the large windows above the front door. The tension was thick, but she could tell it wasn't animosity towards each other that had them so upset.

"We need to figure out how to defend ourselves without any abilities." Tahlia told them.

"We don't have time. We need to see if Whitley can communicate with the Evolved through the rest of the Old Immortals." Dorian replied.

"I will not put her in danger Dorian, don't ask me to." Tahlia said, her voice choking out as she held back tears.

"It won't put her in danger. She has been talking to them the whole time." Dorian scoffed.

"You don't know what those things will do. They know they can kill her. They can infect her. They'll do it without hesitation." Tahlia said.

Whitley had heard enough. She stood and cleared her throat.

The three Old Immortals turned and stared at her as she made her way down the stairs. When she came to the bottom, she stood before them squaring her shoulders.

"I'm an adult. I want to help. I have to help. I got to come back because they want me to help." Whitley told them. "Tell me what I need to do."

Romulus stepped forward and placed a hand on each of her shoulders.

"We need you to reach out to the other Old Immortals and try to get a message to the Evolved. The Maladies are out there, in Benton." Romulus told her.

"What do you mean they're in Benton?" Whitley asked as alarms went off in her head.

"Honey, they're toying with us, trying to draw me out. I don't think they know yet that I am not the vessel. Soon, they'll have infected the entire town." Tahlia said quietly.

"If they're infecting the town, what will happen to the people there?" Whitley asked with concern.

"They're already killing each other." Dorian told her.

Whitley put a hand over her heart. She thought of the families she'd seen there. The quaint downtown area, overrun by violence and murder. She nodded her head at them before closing her eyes to reach out.

She found herself face to face with Marcellus. He was looking at her as though waiting for her to speak.

"Marcellus, we have to tell the Evolved to return. They must get Keira somewhere safe, but they have to come back. If they don't thousands of people will die at the hands of the Maladies." Whitley told him.

He stared blankly for a moment as though in shock. He shook his head quickly and turned on his heel. Whitley watched as Marcellus disappeared as he walked away. She took a deep breath and waited. She didn't have to wait long.

Marcellus returned with Rance and Lucien. Whitley watched them speaking hurriedly as they approached.

"Whitley, you must know that we would love to tell you everything will be alright, but we can't see everything." Rance told her patiently.

"I'm not asking for reassurance, I'm asking you to get a message to the Evolved. You have to tell them to come home. They've been here for a month! We need them to come stop the Maladies. None of us have the power to defend *the innocent people of Benton." Whitley replied with frustration.*

"The Evolved cannot return until they've spoken with the Creator. They will be with him soon." Lucien said quietly.

"Why do I feel like you're not telling me something? What do you know that you're not saying?" Whitley demanded.

Marcellus began to speak but Lucien gave him a stern look, stopping him from saying what was on the tip of his tongue. Whitley had heard enough. She wasn't going to be the go-between for the Old Immortals if they were going to keep things from her.

"Alright, I see how it is. Well, I'm done. If you're not going to help me when you obviously can, why should I help you?" Whitley asked with her arms crossed over her chest.

The Old Immortals exchanged a look before Rance nodded at both Marcellus and Lucien. Whitey hoped that was a good sign and decided to press them further.

"Seriously, I'll leave and I won't even feel bad about it." Whitley baited them.

"While we know you are bluffing, we agree that you need to know what is happening. You have been a faithful and useful agent of the Creator, we owe you this much." Lucien told her.

He stepped forward and touched the tips of his index fingers to her temples. Whitley felt a searing pain explode through her skull. She tried to pull away but seemed to be cemented in place.

When she opened her eyes, she was surrounded by fire in the remnants of a brick building. She felt the wind rush around her and saw lightening flash overhead. The ground began to rumble. She turned around to see Thatcher standing amongst the ruined building.

"Thatcher!" Whitley said as she rushed forward.

He didn't respond, he didn't even see her. Whitley realized that she was not really there, she was just a witness. Thatcher smiled slightly as the thunder boomed around him.

"That's my girl." He said with a grin.

Whitley looked for Hadley amongst the rubble. She saw her sister standing near the edge of the fire.

Whitley caught some movement out of the corner of her eye and whipped around quickly to see eight figures lope through the fire unscathed. The Maladies. Whitley began to shout a warning before remembering that no one would hear her. She saw a small figure standing before the Maladies, ready to face them. There, with her hands on her hips was Keira.

The light flashed again, the pain was excruciating and she found herself face to face with Lucien once again.

"What was that?" Whitley said as she staggered backward.

"The reason Keira cannot go somewhere safe." Marcellus replied.

"You expect a little girl to fight those monsters?" Whitley almost shrieked the question.

"It's not what we expect, it's what has to happen." Rance told her.

Whitley whipped her head back and forth looking at all three of the Old Immortals standing before her. They were serious.

"So what about the people in Benton? Will you at least tell the Evolved that they need to return home?" Whitley asked desperately.

The Old Immortals exchanged a look and shrugged.

"They are meeting with the Creator as we speak. He is preparing them for what is to come. They cannot leave yet." Lucien told her almost apologetically.

With that, Whitley was standing in the foyer of her home again. Her family looked at her expectantly, all she could do was shrug her shoulders and hang her head. She spent the next few minutes explaining what had happened.

"It makes sense that she would have to face them." Dorian said. "They can't kill her."

Whitley stared blankly at Dorian for a moment before looking at her mother. "What if they take her the way they took you? What if they torture her? She's just a child!"

Tahlia looked at her with fear in her eyes, it was clear she had no response to her daughters concerns. Whitley almost saw the memories passing through her mother's mind as she thought about what had happened to her in that abandoned outbuilding.

Chapter Thirty-Eight: Hadley

She came out of the bedroom to find everyone else waiting for her. When Thatcher saw her he smiled widely and tossed her a blueberry muffin. She caught it and peeled the paper off.

"Make sure you eat enough. There's scrambled eggs and toast too." Malcolm told her.

Hadley nodded, her mouth full of blueberry deliciousness. She sat down next to Thatcher and scooped a helping of scrambled eggs onto her plate.

"I wish there were pancakes." Keira said sadly.

"You do huh?" Malcolm asked her with a wink.

A plate stacked high with pancakes materialized before them. Hadley watched Keira's eyes light up with excitement as

Nora put a few on her daughter's plate and cut them up.

"This is cool. Are you my uncle too Malcolm?" Keira said through a mouthful of pancakes.

Malcolm smiled widely at her. "You bet!"

Thatcher and Kerr helped themselves to some more food. Once everyone had eaten their fill, the meal before them disappeared. They sat in silence for a few moments before anyone moved.

"The Creator is waiting for you." Malcolm told them.

Hadley took Thatcher's hand and squeezed. They stood together, followed by Kerr, Nora and Keira. Thatcher clasped Malcolm's hand and pulled him in for a hug.

"It was good to see you." Thatcher told him.

"You too man." Malcolm replied.

"Thank you for everything." Hadley said.

"Anything for you guys. I mean that." Malcolm told them.

Once they said their goodbyes, the Evolved took a step through a door that led to another staircase. They began their climb, and found themselves in the Great Hall in what seemed like seconds.

It was beautiful and flooded with light. Pillars lined the exterior walls and a large marble table dominated the center of the room. Large marble chairs with lush purple upholstery surrounded the table. The hall was silent but not in an empty or lonely way, the silence felt comfortable and warm. The paused at the entry, unsure of where to go.

"Come, sit." A voice said.

They looked at each other for only a moment before taking their seats around the table. Hadley felt the cold marble of the table and the warm comfort of the chair. She had been surprised at how easy it was to pull the marble chair away from the table. Even Keira had no trouble moving hers.

As soon as they were all seated they were bathed in a bright light and the Creator appeared at the head of the table.

Hadley didn't know what she had expected him to look like, but she wasn't disappointed. His eyes were a kind and warm deep brown. His silver hair fell down over his shoulders in wavy wisps. He smiled widely at those gathered around his table.

"Welcome." He said with a smile.

Hadley could tell the rest of the Evolved were just as speechless as she now found herself to be. The only one who didn't appear to be in awe of their host was Keira. The little girl jumped off her chair and ran to the Creator with open arms. He chuckled and scooped her up with ease.

"Hello little one! It's good to see you." The Creator said with a hearty laugh.

"Hi. It's good to meet you." Keira told him.

The Creator set her down and patted her head lovingly. She skipped back to her seat at the table and climbed back into her chair.

"So, I hear you want some answers." The Creator said looking at Thatcher.

Hadley was about to interject but Thatcher held up a hand to stop her.

"Yes. In the last five years we've put up with a lot of stuff. We've lost people we care about, we got some of them back and we've literally killed the devil. We've been chasing down the evil crap Absalom left in the world and now we have to face his minions." Thatcher paused before continuing. "They got to me, I tried to kill my friends and family, I actually killed Hadley and we can't even beat them."

Hadley reached over and took Thatcher's hand and squeezed. She wanted to reassure him that he wasn't alone in this and that the answers were right in front of them. She had to believe that the Creator would give them guidance.

"Who says you can't beat them?" The Creator asked.

"Well we haven't scared them so far. All they have to do is touch one of us. They tortured my mother!" Hadley exclaimed.

"No, you're right, the four of you don't scare them. But that doesn't mean they can't be beaten." The Creator replied.

"With all due respect, what is that supposed mean?" Kerr asked.

"Why do you think I put the spirit of hope into the sphere with the Maladies?" The Creator asked. "I knew that the only thing that would give mankind the ability to carry on despite the presence of such evil in the world would be to give them hope."

Hadley looked over at Nora and Kerr, she was waiting for them to catch on. Hadley was slowly realizing exactly what the Creator was telling them; the only thing that could stop the Maladies was hope. Hadley didn't have to wait for them to catch up because Keira spoke first.

"It's me. I have to stop them." Keira said with a confidence that belied her age.

"What? No." Nora said, her voice rising in terror.

"I know she is your daughter, but she is also carrying a part of me within her. The spirit of hope came from within me, that spirit manifested itself in Tahlia all those years ago and now, Keira carries it within her." The Creator told them.

"Did Tahlia have a life before the sphere broke?" Kerr asked suddenly.

"She did, but it wasn't much of a life. She was a good woman who made poor decisions. I'll let her tell you the rest of the story. She now knows who she was. The fact that the spirit of hope chose her is a perfect example of how there are no lost causes and every life can be worth more." The Creator shared.

"And Keira? Why was she chosen to be the vessel?" Nora asked.

"Because she is a child that came to your family in a time of great terror and desperation. You weren't ready for her, but her existence gave you all a reason to believe in the future." He told her.

Hadley sat quietly, everything the Creator had said made sense, though she couldn't help but wonder what poor decisions her mother had made before she was chosen to be the vessel. Another thought occurred to her, she had so many questions about Whitley's return.

"Sorry to change the subject, but what about Whitley? Why did she get to come back? I thought we had to be one person in order for us to fulfill our prophecy." Hadley said with uncertainty.

"Ah, there are some things that must be left to play out, and I'm afraid that is one of them. I cannot tell you why she was able to return or what the future holds for her. I can tell you that your sister was brought back to you because prophecies are fickle. The prophecy was more about your abilities than it was about your physical body. After all, your mother did give birth to two children." The Creator smiled at her.

Hadley wasn't sure what to think about the cryptic answer she received. She had to believe that Whitley had returned for a reason, and now she knew that one day they would find out what that reason was.

Chapter Thirty-Nine: Nora

Nora had been listening patiently and trying not to freak out about her daughter joining the impending battle. Keira was sitting in her chair listening intently to everything the Creator had to say. The connection her daughter felt with him had been instantaneous.

"So if the Evolved can't beat them, how is Keira supposed to fight them? She's only four." Nora interjected.

"Ah, there's the question I was waiting for. Yes, your daughter is just a child, but she holds an ancient spirit within her that will guide her through the battle." The Creator told them.

"So she's going to beat them and then what?" Thatcher asked.

"Oh, she isn't going to beat them, she can't." The Creator gave them all a look of concern. "You know they can't leave your world until the New Era right?"

Nora exchanged a look with the other Evolved. Clearly they didn't know that or they wouldn't have been looking for a way to win a battle against the Maladies.

"Won't beating the Maladies bring the New Era about?" Hadley asked in confusion.

The Creator laughed loudly. Nora was trying desperately not to get irritated with him, but it was getting more difficult the longer it took to tell them what was expected of them and what would happen to her daughter when she faced the Maladies.

"Why is that funny? Can't you just tell us what you need us to do?" Nora asked.

"I apologize, I truly didn't realize just how little you knew about your mission." The Creator said, calming his laughter. "I need you to prepare the world for my return."

Nora was taken aback by this information. The Creator was going to return to their world? Was he going to walk around with everyone? Was he talking about creating utopia?

"Yes Nora, that is essentially what will happen when the New Era begins." The Creator told her with a grin.

She didn't even have time to register that she hadn't spoken aloud. Nora looked at the being who had created everything she had ever known. She thought they were supposed to eradicate evil from the world in order to usher in the New Era.

"When do you plan to return?" Thatcher asked incredulously.

"Ah, only time will tell. But now is not the right time. The world is not ready for me yet. Absalom and his lackey's have burned their way into the hearts and minds of my people for too long. I cannot return until they are ready." The Creator replied with a hint of sadness.

"So how do I make them stop?" Keira asked quietly.

"Now that is an excellent question." The Creator chuckled. "We need to bind them temporarily so they cannot infect anyone and do not remember who they are. We cannot eradicate them from our world yet, but when the binding begins to wear off, it will be time for the final battle."

Nora shook her head suddenly, trying desperately to grasp onto what the Creator was telling them. They had to perform a binding on the Maladies? Were they supposed to perform some kind of Wiccan ritual now? She looked at the others around the table and found their faces to be just as confused as hers.

"Keira will know how to do the binding. In order to bind them, we must restore the balance. With all the evil they have done and Absalom did before them, mankind is beginning to feel the hopelessness they sow. The binding will suspend the Maladies within their own minds." The Creator told them. "They all have to be present in order for the binding to work. They must all be bound at the same time."

"How will we get them all together?" Thatcher asked.

"Sadly, that won't be as difficult as you may think. They are currently wreaking havoc on your home. Benton is under siege." He told them evenly.

Nora gasped and looked at Hadley in alarm. The girls exchanged a knowing look before either could say anything. They had to get home. Their family was there, defenseless.

"How long have they been attacking?" Kerr asked.

"A few days. They have been trying to reach Tahlia. They believe she still holds the spirit of hope within her." He said sadly.

"So you're telling me that my mother has been a sitting duck in a house in the middle of South Dakota just waiting for these disgusting creatures to attack and kill her? My sister, Dorian, Romulus and my mother

are all powerless against the Maladies."
Hadley nearly shouted at the Creator.

"I understand why you are upset, but you
came to speak with me. You needed to learn
about your mission. You needed to
understand how important it is for Keira to
be there." He replied.

"Why didn't you give this information to
the Virtues? Why didn't they even
remember their home?" Hadley demanded.

"Sadly, I had to remove certain memories
for fear that Absalom or his minions would
find a way to extract that information. I
removed the memory from all of the Old
Immortals once the prophecies were given.
I couldn't exactly have Absalom returning
to Eternity with his crew could I? Think of
the innocent souls that are resting here.
Think of the monstrous souls that are
trapped below the mountain. Just imagine
what he could have done." He said in a
strained voice.

Nora could tell the Creator truly cared for
his creations and wanted to stress the

importance of their involvement in the coming battle. He was depending on them. It was their job to ensure the safety of the vessel and their job to help her bind the Maladies. As much as they wanted to there to protect their family and the citizens of Benton, their place was here. If they hadn't traveled to Eternity, they would have tried to take on the Maladies on their own.

Although it went against every instinct Nora had, she knew what they needed to do. They needed to dive right into the battle. She needed to allow her daughter to risk her safety in order to save the world.

Chapter Forty: Keira

She had tried to listen to everything the adults were talking about but she didn't understand it all. In her mind something strange was happening. She could feel the light within her trying to tell her something important, so she listened.

The light was asking for permission. It knew she wasn't ready to fight any bad guys. The light wanted to do it for her. The more she listened to what the light was telling her the more she understood what it wanted. It wanted to take her over, but it wanted her to be okay with it.

Keira closed her eyes and agreed. She knew she would be able to watch everything happen and she would remember it all. But she wouldn't have to be the one to make the decisions. She was scared and knew that if she tried to be brave enough to face the Maladies she would probably get people killed.

A strange warmth spread over her body. It felt like drinking hot cocoa on a cold winter day. The heat started in her chest and slowly spread through her body until she was warm all over. Opening her eyes, she glanced at her skin, it seemed to be glowing faintly. She looked at her parents and at the other two Evolved. Everything seemed to slide into focus and became sharper and more vibrant with each passing second.

"Keira?" Nora's voice was slightly panicked.

"It's alright mommy. I'll be back." Keira told her mother before giving herself over completely to the spirit of hope.

"Keira? Can you hear me?" Nora asked urgently. "Kerr, her eyes. They've turned blue."

"I don't mean to alarm you, but Keira has let me take over for the time being."

Everyone stared at her with open mouths except for the Creator. He smiled at her with pride.

"I am Elpis." She told them.

Chapter Forty-One: Elpis

"Where is my daughter?" Nora demanded.

"She is here. But she is letting me take over until the battle is won. She is not yet familiar with the abilities afforded the vessel of hope." Elpis replied.

She looked around at the Evolved. She had watched them grow and change through the eyes of Tahlia but had not had the opportunity to speak with anyone herself in centuries. Her eyes settled on Hadley.

"Your mother is a brave woman. You should be proud of the sacrifices she made to keep hope alive in your world. Though I know it is still difficult for you to understand, and you probably want to tell me off, it is important for you to know that everything she did was for the future of your world." Elpis told her.

"Thank you. You're right, it isn't easy to understand. But, I'm talking to an ancient spirit inside the body of a four year old girl. So...there's that." Hadley said slowly.

Elpis felt laughter bubble up inside her and she let it out. It felt strange to communicate through a child, but she couldn't help the age of the vessel. She had not planned on leaving Tahlia before the child was ready. She looked to Kerr and Nora next.

"I would not have joined your daughter until she was older, but the moment the Maladies took Tahlia, we knew it had to happen quickly. Tahlia fought it as long as she could to protect your daughter, but in the end she knew what she had to do. I had to leave her and enter the next vessel. I cannot survive in your world without the vessel. I cannot guarantee that your daughter will not suffer under my care, but I can guarantee you that she will not perish. She is the final vessel." She told Keira's worried parents.

Kerr closed his mouth quickly, obviously still in shock. Elpis wondered how strange it must be for him to hear her mature and soft voice coming from the body of his young daughter. Elpis looked to the Creator, her Father. She bowed her head to him in reverence. She had not been in his presence in centuries.

"It is time for us to bind the evils that threaten your world." Elpis told them. "Come, we haven't much time."

The others looked at each other with concern. Thatcher had taken Hadley's hand and Kerr was supporting his shocked wife. The four of them cautiously approached Elpis.

"Thank you for your hospitality Father. I shall see you again in the New Era." Elpis told the Creator.

"Yes, you all will. I am proud of each of you and look forward to the day we are reunited." The Creator said as he faded away.

Elpis looked to the Evolved and held out Keira's little hand. They were hesitant but they knew they needed to return to their world. As she took Kerr's hand in her own, she thought back to the day she was released from the sphere. It was the last time she had been able to speak as herself. It was the day she had given herself completely to the first vessel.

She still remembered the day she claimed Tahlia from a life of ill-repute. The woman she had been was nothing compared to the woman she became. Her heart was pure; she had been forced into her lifestyle to survive. She had done what she'd had to in the hope of securing a future for her unborn child. Keira was lucky to have been spared a life such as Tahlia's. And Elpis had given Tahlia the gift of erasing the memory of her life before. Some things were better forgotten.

In an instant they were standing in the center of Benton. Elpis didn't need to find doorways to and from Eternity, she could create them. A loud crash behind them caught their attention. They turned in time to see an old brick building crumble.

"Come, they are near." Elpis told them as she took off at a run. Keira's small legs slowed her progress as she tried to climb over piles of rubble.

The stench of death and decay told her the Maladies had been destroying the city for days. As they poured onto the main road, Elpis saw the bodies lying all around. She was filled with sorrow at the sight, more innocent lives taken because of evil and corruption.

"All these people..." Hadley said sadly.

"This is our fault." Thatcher said in frustration.

"No. This began long before you were born. This is not about getting to you or stopping me. For them, this is about destroying the world the Creator holds dearly." Elpis told them.

Kerr knelt beside a body and checked for a pulse. He must have found one because he began trying to wake the unconscious man in front of him.

"I have to try to save some of these people and get them out of here before it gets any uglier." Kerr told them desperately.

Elpis nodded. "Yes. You and Nora must remove as many survivors as you can and try to heal their wounds. We will engage the Maladies."

They agreed with the plan and quickly parted ways. Nora and Kerr would find few survivors, but the humans must be saved whenever possible. Hadley and Thatcher followed Elpis as she took off at a run towards the location of the Maladies.

They came around a corner and found themselves face to face with the Maladies. Thatcher instinctively threw up a wall of fire along the lines where the foundation lay in ruins. They were boxed in by the fire, trapping the Maladies with them.

Rage had taken a special interest in Thatcher and was circling him like a lion stalking its prey. Elpis knew that Thatcher had dealt with the aftermath of this particular evil before. She would not make him endure it again.

Thunder crashed overhead as Hadley caught sight of what was happening near Thatcher. The ground rumbled, the wind whipped around them, the lightening flashed and crackled in the night sky.

"That's my girl." Thatcher said with a grin.

Elpis stepped forward to face the Maladies.

"Oh this is a surprise." Malice said when she saw Elpis.

"Malice, it is time for you to stand down." Elpis commanded.

"Yeah, I don't think so." Malice said as she laughed. "How's a wittle girl like you gonna stop me?"

Elpis sighed deeply and shot a beam of light from her hand in the direction of her enemy. Malice yelped as the light hit her shoulder. Malice looked at her wound and hissed at the white burn that would never heal. The momentary distraction gave

Hadley enough time to sneak behind her and hit her with a blast of energy that sent Malice forward where she fell splayed across the rubble.

Her light had a calming and inspiring effect on humans; as a result she was often misrepresented as a muse. They were entirely different beings, but she understood the confusion. Her light was not used to inspire artists, but great acts that restored faith in humanity. Hope can touch even the darkest souls; it left a mark on the body, and burned the soul. This light was especially painful to those who had no hope left in them; their soul can no longer endure the purest light. Such was the case for the Maladies.

"Don't think it will be that easy Elpis." Malice scoffed.

"No, it will be much easier." Elpis replied grimly.

She took in her surroundings again. Hadley was trying to battle with the Maladies from afar. It never ceased to amaze Elpis how fervently humans fought against what the Creator had planned for them. The Evolved should not be trying to fight the Maladies, they should be trying to corral them so she could bind them. Thatcher was in danger; he was letting his personal vendetta against Rage cloud his judgment.

It was time for her to take control of the battle.

Chapter Forty-Two: Thatcher

Rage was circling him. It made his stomach turn to see the hunger in the eyes of the evil standing before him. He watched him wearily, aware for the first time that Hadley was losing her temper.

The thunder and lightning crashed around them, striking the ground around the ruined building. He saw Keira's slight frame step forward to face Rage and he instinctively moved to protect her but found himself frozen in place by an unseen force.

He glanced over his shoulder to see Hadley standing with her arms folded triumphantly as she held him in place. Thatcher looked back to where Elpis had been standing. She was now surrounded by Rage, Avarice and Disease.

They circled her with ill-contained glee. The idea of infecting a child clearly appealed to them. Apparently they hadn't witnessed the exchange between Elpis and Malice. Elpis turned to keep an eye on each of them, bobbing and weaving at lightening speeds when they tried to touch her. They couldn't infect her but she wasn't going to let them find out so quickly. Thatcher watched as Chaos approached, ignoring the little girl and heading straight for him.

Thatcher struggled against the force that held him, silently cursing Hadley for being so protective. He pushed against her again only to stumble forward unexpectedly. He glanced over his shoulder at Hadley to find her writhing in agony on the ground. Pain stood over her, leaning down and touching her with just one finger.

No. This was not going to happen. Thatcher turned from Chaos and took off towards Pain and Hadley throwing fireballs as he went. Pain was hardly distracted by the fire raining down on him. He smiled evilly at Thatcher as he approached.

"Don't touch her again." Thatcher said through gritted teeth. Something was happening to him; the abilities he had inherited from killing Absalom were threatening to surface. "You like a little pain do you?"

Thatcher slashed a hand through the air and blood spilled from a gash in Pain's stomach. The Malady grunted but healed instantly. Thatcher reached deep within himself when he saw Hadley still writhing on the ground. He used an ability he had never used before; he sent Pain flying towards Elpis without lifting a finger.

Nora and Kerr had materialized near Hadley moments later. Thatcher was relieved to see them. They instantly jumped into battle. Nora grabbed a pipe as she ran towards Malice who had woken and begun slinking her way towards them.

Kerr knelt next to Hadley trying to heal what Pain had done to her. Only Hope could break the hold of a Malady. Kerr took off to help Nora, leaving Hadley lying on the ground in the fetal position.

Nora made her way back to Hadley once Kerr was distracting Malice. Thatcher was relieved to see Hadley melt from view as Nora cloaked her from the battle.

He looked at Elpis to see her attempting to gather the Maladies in one place. When he looked back to his friends, Thatcher had lost sight of Nora and Kerr. He whipped his head around frantically to find Kerr lying on the ground as Nora wielded a broken pipe trying to protect him from Malice.

He looked back at Chaos. She hadn't touched him, why had everything gone so nuts all at once? She grinned and winked at him.

"What did you do?" Thatcher demanded.

"I can create chaos wherever I go, I don't have to touch anyone. Chaos doesn't generally come from just one person after all." She replied with a laugh.

Thatcher watched her with disgust as she climbed up on the crumbled remains of a chimney at the center of the battle. He saw her perch atop the pile of bricks next to Vanity. He shook his head at Vanity calmly filing her nails. Rolling his eyes he sent a few fireballs in their direction and couldn't help but chuckle when they yelped in surprise.

Thatcher couldn't decide which way to go first. He looked back and forth between where his fiancé lay and his friends for a moment before he tried to move. He found himself frozen in fear. He couldn't move. He didn't want to move. If he moved, something bad might happen. His heart was beating as though it would burst from his chest and he was sweating profusely. What was happening to him?

He whirled around to find a frail, wide-eyed man smiling maniacally at him. Of course, Panic. He took a deep, calming breath and tried desperately to fight against the anxiety that rose inside him. He had already been touched by Panic, why not go all out? He swung a punch at his terrified face, hitting him square in the nose. Panic screamed in a very feminine manner and fainted. Thatcher shook his head, did he actually just faint?

He didn't have time to fully appreciate the humor in the situation as he ran towards Hadley.

Thatcher had just enough time to scoop Hadley up and run. She was whimpering in his arms. Even without the constant touch of the Malady, Hadley was still in agonizing pain. He couldn't just set her down to be attacked again but the others needed him too. He felt the anxiety begin to tighten his chest again as he tried to determine his next course of action.

Nora practically shouted in his head. "We need to get them over to Keir—I mean Elpis. They have to surround her in order for her to bind them."

Thatcher made eye contact with his cousin and nodded his head in understanding. He hoisted Hadley back into his arms and moved closer to Nora. Malice had left them alone but was still searching for them. It was clear that Nora was using her abilities to hide herself and her husband.

Before Thatcher could reach Nora, Chaos and Malice noticed his presence. He was really starting to get worried. He didn't know what to do. He tried to push the fear and panic from his mind, but it was crippling. He slowly let Hadley down to the ground. She was slipping in and out of consciousness as all her muscles continued to contract in the constant torture Pain had inflicted on her.

As he saw her beautiful face wrinkled in discomfort he found what was left of the calm he so desperately needed and hoisted her back up into his arms. He closed the gap between himself and Nora in a few moments and laid Hadley gently beside Kerr. He took one look at his friend and realized he had suffered a blow; a deep gash bled freely on his forehead.

"I'm going to try to round them up." Thatcher said, trying to hide the fear in his voice.

"No you're not. Don't be an idiot. They can't see us right now. We already tried to join the battle. Look at us now." Nora shook her head and looked at her daughter. "If Elpis is the only one here, they'll automatically go to her. We might as well realize that the Creator was right; Elpis has to do this. Without us."

Thatcher couldn't believe what he was hearing. Nora was actually letting her daughter be bait and fight this battle on her own. He knew Keira wasn't exactly home but this was still just a little girl. He grudgingly sat down and tried to soothe Hadley.

Soon enough, Nora's guess had proven correct as the Maladies began to swarm around Elpis. He caught one glimpse of the little girls face and saw the triumph written all over it.

Chapter Forty-Three: Elpis

She smiled at the Maladies as they began to swarm around her like parasites ready to latch on to an unknowing victim.

"I've been waiting for this." She told them.

Her skin began to glow and her eyes lit up with an ethereal blue light. A moment of recognition crossed the faces of the Maladies as they saw her for who she really was.

"Well, well, well, did we finally succeed in destroying your vessel?" Malice asked with a sneer.

"Not quite." Elpis told her.

"Looks like you've found a new home either way." Avarice said in her condescending tone.

"I have. And it's time for you all to do the same. You've caused enough trouble for mankind." Elpis told them.

The Maladies laughed together. It was clear they did not think she had the power to do anything to them. She thought back to the time she had spent in the sphere with them. Their hatred towards the Creator, Old Immortals and mankind had led them to this point. Their hatred had destroyed them. Now they wore their worst sins as a constant reminder of the hatred that brought them here.

"You can't kill us. Only the Creator can destroy us." Vanity said sounding for all the world like a valley girl.

"Oh, I'm not going to kill you. I'm just going to put a damper on your plans for a while." Elpis replied.

The Maladies exchanged a look that told her she was starting to scare them. Good. They needed to understand that they were done. All eight of the Maladies stood around her in a circle just as she needed them to. She closed her eyes and focused deep within herself.

Elpis let the power within her build, releasing it just as it reached its peak. The light burst forth hitting each of them square in the chest. Their angered cries filled her ears as the light burned into their bodies. The light enveloped each of them from head to toe before erupting in a million different directions.

The light reached out and touched every soul in the world. She knew the tiny seed of hope she planted in each human being would be all that was needed to neutralize the evil emanating from the Maladies.

Soon, the light seemed to suck back in to the Maladies then back to its home inside Keira. The evil beings around her slowly drifted to the ground. Elpis looked at their lifeless forms, they wouldn't wake for many years.

Chapter Forty-Four: Kerr

Kerr had regained consciousness when the entire ruined building was bathed in the purest light he had ever seen. He didn't entirely remember what had happened to him, he decided he'd have to ask Nora. Before he could say anything to anyone, the fire around them dissipated and they were left in the relative darkness of downtown Benton.

"Holy crap. That was the coolest thing I've ever seen." Thatcher said as he made his way over the rubble.

Beside him, Hadley sat up and looked herself over. When she decided she was alright, she rose and followed Thatcher to examine the motionless bodies lying in an array around Keira.

"Nora?" Kerr asked.

"Hmm?" She replied, still gripping a pipe in her hands.

"Why am I bleeding?" He asked as he gingerly touched his throbbing head.

"I hit you." She said simply.

"What? Why?" Kerr asked in disbelief.

"Malice touched you. You freaked out. As soon as you rounded on me and started acting like a macho douchebag I grabbed this and whacked you over the head." Nora told him tossing aside the pipe she'd been brandishing.

Kerr laughed in spite of the nauseating pain in his head. Nora never ceased to surprise him and this was no exception. When faced with a merciless enemy and a suddenly violent and cruel husband she chose to simply eliminate part of the problem. His amusement quickly turned to concern as he wondered what he had done to warrant the crack on the head.

"Don't worry, I didn't let you close enough to do anything stupid. It wasn't you anyway. Sorry for the headache though." Nora said as she offered him her hand.

As Nora helped him stand he felt slightly dizzy, she must have hit him pretty hard. "Remind me not to tick you off alright?" He grimaced.

They made their way over to the others and found themselves looking at the Maladies as they must have appeared before they allowed themselves to become corrupted by their hatred. Disease and Pain no longer showed physical manifestations of the evil within.

"What happens to them now?" Hadley asked. With the Maladies bound, Pain could not infect her anymore.

"I will spread them out. They will be John and Jane Doe's lying comatose in hospitals for a long time. When they wake, they will start to look for one another. That will be the sign the Creator needs to return." Elpis told them.

Kerr nodded. He still wasn't entirely sure what they were supposed to do with their lives while they waited for the Maladies to wake up, but it felt good knowing they weren't going to hurt anyone for a while. He didn't know what the future would bring, but he knew they could face it. In that moment, Kerr had resolved to accept whatever challenges they faced. He felt his body begin to vibrate from his toes to the top of his head. He felt himself lift off the ground as he embraced the future, fulfilling his prophecy.

"Whoop! It's about time!" Thatcher called out as Kerr came back to the ground.

Kerr laughed at Thatcher's excitement. All of the Evolved had finally fulfilled their prophecies. They had fulfilled the expectations the Creator had set for them long before they were born.

He looked around him, realizing for the first time that he was standing in the remains of his store. He hadn't had time to do much with it, but now it was gone altogether. The building had been empty for at least a year but it had been his home at one point. He looked beyond the boundaries of what used to be a building to see that a few neighboring buildings were in a similar state.

He made his way into the street taking in the damage that the citizens of Benton had been led to do. He and Nora had managed to find only fifty survivors lying in the street. He was heartbroken that they'd been just seconds too late for many of them.

He could only hope that most of the citizens of their small town had gotten away with their lives. Kerr desperately needed to check on his mother and stepfather, but knew it would have to wait until they'd spoken with the Virtues and Whitley.

The crisp night air was filled with a deafening silence. It was almost as though the people had simply abandoned one another in order to save themselves. He felt so much sorrow for the innocent people who lost their lives to their friends and neighbors.

"They can't do this anymore right?" Kerr asked Elpis as she came to stand beside him.

"Not directly no. The evil they represent will still be in your world but they cannot turn people into something they're not. It will be similar to when they were trapped in the Underworld. They will absorb the negative energy of the people who invite those evils into their hearts. They won't be conscious, they won't know they're doing it." She replied.

Kerr felt Nora take his hand; he squeezed in response. They turned back to the wreckage of the Book Nook and made their way back to the Maladies. Hadley and Thatcher came to join them.

"I need to take them now. When I return I need to speak with the Virtues, then I will give control back to Keira." Elpis told them before she disappeared in a flash of light.

Kerr looked at the other Evolved. His head was pounding and he needed to sit down. Nora and Thatcher supported his weight as he started to collapse.

"We'd better get back to the house. If we've been gone for a month we need to fill the others in on what has happened." Nora said calmly.

He felt the now familiar pull in the pit of his stomach as Nora transported them back to their house. The Evolved found themselves standing in the entryway of the house. Kerr lost his grip on Thatcher and Nora and fell to the ground with a crash. In seconds, the Old Immortals and Whitley surrounded them. They all held some manner of weapon at the ready.

"Whoa. It's just us." Thatcher said with his hands in the air.

Whitley threw her crossbow to the ground and ran to her sister. She pulled her into a tight hug before releasing her to look at them all.

"It's about time! Do you know what's happening out there?" She demanded.

Kerr raised a hand from the ground. "Trust me, we know."

Romulus made his way to Kerr and helped him up from the ground. Tahlia came forward and looked at his head.

"What happened to you?" Tahlia asked.

"Nora." Kerr told her with a shrug.

Romulus couldn't hold in his laughter at Kerr's response. He shook as he tried to support his grandson's weight.

"It's not funny. Malice touched him. He turned into a jerk. He said some stupid crap and threatened to kill me. So, I hit him over the head with a pipe." Nora said as she barely controlled her own laughter.

Kerr scowled at them. Romulus and Dorian high-fived Nora. Tahlia helped him to the kitchen and began washing the wound.

"So, you beat them?" Whitley asked.

"Not exactly." Hadley told her.

"Wait." Whitley looked them all over one more time as the panic became evident in her face. "Where's Keira?"

Chapter Forty-Five: Dorian

He had listened as the Evolved told their story. Their time in Eternity had been well spent. He was in awe of their experiences and wished with all his heart that he could remember the wonders his home held.

When the Evolved had detailed their attempts to intervene in the fight between the Maladies and Elpis, he appreciated their zealousness but was pleased that they let go in the end. He had learned through the years that putting faith in the plan would pay off in the end.

The binding of the Maladies gave him some comfort. Dorian didn't entirely understand why Tahlia hadn't been able to bind them. He was glad everyone was safe, but he felt confused about what to do next.

They had removed all threats to mankind but the Creator had not returned. He had no idea when the Creator would return or if he would be alive to see it.

"You will." A voice startled him from his thoughts.

He looked up to find Keira standing in the middle of the library. It took him only a moment to realize it wasn't Keira staring back at him but Elpis, the spirit of hope.

"I'm mortal now. I won't be around forever." Dorian told her.

"Yes, that is true. You have fulfilled the mission the Creator tasked you with and you will now age as a mortal. But you are only about forty by the standards of man. The Creator will return long before your mortal body expires." Elpis replied.

Dorian blinked at her for a moment as he processed what he had just been told. He would still be here for the Evolved when the Creator returns. He would still be here for the final battle.

"Something has been troubling me and I hope you're able to answer my question. Why was the battle so easy?" Dorian asked curiously.

"Because this was never about the Maladies. They were simply a bump in the road. This has been about me." Elpis replied simply. "While I hadn't intended to take up residence in this vessel for many years, I had to move sometime. Your world was teetering on a ledge between the future the Creator has intended and a future filled with hopelessness."

Dorian nodded his head as he looked at her brilliant blue eyes. "So when you sent hope through the world, you pulled us back from the ledge?"

"Essentially, yes." She said. "Evil is infectious, but hope is contagious. People will feel the hope in each other and begin to move forward and heal from the harm that has been done to them. The people who were infected by the Maladies will not be charged for their crimes. No one will remember, not even them. As far as the citizens of Benton are concerned, there was an F5 tornado that struck the town leaving significant damage in its wake."

Dorian wasn't sure he fully understood. "So why weren't you able to bind the Maladies prior to Tahlia losing hope?"

"I had been a part of Tahlia for so long she had forgotten that I wasn't a separate entity. Anytime I tried to speak to her, she brushed it off as her own random thoughts. She is aging. As people mature their hearts and minds are less open to things that seem impossible." Elpis said with a hint of sadness.

"So you needed a younger vessel, one who would be more open to the possibilities you bring to the world." Dorian said slowly.

"Basically, yes. There is more to it than that. Keira was chosen for a reason. She gave your family hope in desperate times." Elpis told him.

The library door opened and Dorian was pleased to find Romulus and Tahlia shuffle in to the room.

GROWING hope

"I'm glad you're here. I wanted to speak with you all. I have a message from the Creator." Elpis said.

They sat on the edge of their seats awaiting the message. Elpis pulled a worn book from the pocket of Keira's jacket. She handed it to Dorian. He looked down at the book of prophecies in his hand.

"There's more. You are all going to be mortal soon enough, but you are still the guides for the Creators plan." Elpis told them.

"I don't understand." Tahlia told her.

Elpis gave her a kind smile; it reminded Dorian of a grandmother looking lovingly at her grandchild. He knew the connection between the spirit and her original vessel was still strong.

"The Creator has given you more prophecies. Three more. They will help you guide the Evolved as they help the Creator in the final battle." Elpis said.

"The Evolved, and their children after them, will help to shape the world in the New Era. There will be much to rebuild and much for the people left in the world to learn. It will not happen overnight." Elpis told them.

"What do you mean the people left in the world?" Dorian asked apprehensively.

"When the Maladies engage in battle with the Creator, they will destroy people and places without hesitation. There will be an army of people who join ranks with the Maladies of their own accord. The casualties will be staggering in number." Elpis said sadly.

Dorian wished he could say he was surprised. If the damage the Maladies had done to Benton was any indication of what would come, the world was in for a rough ride. He found comfort in the feeling of the leather bound book in his hands. This book had brought them this far and would help them to move on to the next phase.

"These prophecies pertain to the end of the present era. You mustn't share their existence with anyone outside this circle until it is time." Elpis instructed.

"We're expected to keep secrets from the Evolved?" Romulus asked in surprise.

Elpis nodded. "You must. If they know of these prophecies they may be reluctant to move forward with their lives or will look for signs where they do not exist. You may not tell them there are more prophecies; they must live their lives as though their part in the battle is over. In fact, the book will not open until the end is near."

Dorian furrowed his brow and tried to open the book he was holding. It wouldn't budge. He looked at the others in surprise.

"How will we know what to look for if we cannot access the prophecies?" Dorian asked.

"The book will open when it is time." Elpis said. "Now, I must go. You should have plenty of time before the final battle. Enjoy each other, enjoy your lives, and please encourage the Evolved to do the same."

With that, Keira collapsed to the floor. The unearthly glow that had surrounded her was gone. Dorian fell to his knees beside her and touched her head. She appeared to be sleeping peacefully. He lifted her from the floor and carried her to her room.

Chapter Forty-Six: Hadley

2016

She stood in front of the mirror staring at her long white dress. The day had finally come. In less than an hour, she would marry Thatcher. The door opened behind her and Whitley came in followed by Nora.

Her sister and best friend looked beautiful in their coral dresses. Their hair was loosely swept up with long curls falling here and there.

"Don't look so nervous!" Nora told her.

"Yeah, it's not like you haven't been talking about this for the past six months." Whitley chimed in.

"I'm just flustered. Does my make-up look alright?" She asked her sister.

"You look a little splotchy. Let me help." Whitley led Hadley to a chair and grabbed her make-up bag.

Hadley closed her eyes and let her sister work her magic. "How many people are out there?"

"Not many. You said you wanted a small ceremony." Nora reassured her.

"Although, that doesn't count all the secret service agents that are here to protect mom and dad in little old Benton." Whitley told her with a smile in her voice.

"Well, it's not like they don't need to be overly cautious after the last time they were here." Hadley said.

"Yeah, well, it's not every day the President's daughter gets married." Nora laughed.

"Oh Lord!" Hadley said, trying not to change her expression.

"There! Done." Whitley declared.

Hadley looked at herself in the mirror and was much happier with what she saw than she had been minutes before.

"Is mom out there? Why hasn't she come in to see me?" Hadley asked.

"I'll go get her." Nora said as she disappeared through the bedroom door.

"Had, are you alright?" Whitley asked her sister.

"I'm fine. Just ready to get this over with. The whole wedding part is great and all, but I'm looking forward to spending some time with Thatcher away from all the planning and family and secret service." Hadley said.

"About that...Dad is insisting that a few of his agents accompany you on your honeymoon." Whitley told her carefully.

"For real? Thatcher has a whole arsenal of abilities and I can strike people down with lightning whenever I want. What are a couple of guys with guns going to do that we can't already do ourselves?" Hadley asked.

"Well, pay attention to your surroundings for one thing. I'm sure you two are going to be a little pre-occupied." Whitley laughed.

Hadley crossed her arms and pouted. The door opened and her mother came in with Nora. Tahlia caught a glimpse of her daughter sulking and rolled her eyes.

"I take it Whitley told you." Tahlia said.

"Yeah." Hadley replied shortly.

"Well, your father and I feel that it would be best for you to have some added protection while you're on your honeymoon. The head of the secret service agrees with us." Tahlia told her.

"What, now that you're the First Lady you have to be even more overprotective?" Hadley asked.

Tahlia rolled her eyes and grabbed Hadley's veil. Tahlia and Eric had remarried shortly after the Maladies had been subdued. Hadley and Whitley's mother had adjusted to life at the White

House fairly quickly but it was clear she missed her home in South Dakota.

"There. Perfect." Tahlia said as she finished fastening the veil to Hadley's head.

A knock on the door startled Hadley as a secret service agent spoke from the other side.

"Ladies, it's time." He said.

Hadley smiled at her sister and gave Nora a quick squeeze. Tahlia left the room to be escorted to her seat by Thatcher.

Nora and Whitley left to be escorted down the aisle by Kerr and Dorian. The next knock on the door brought Eric to escort his daughter to her soon to be husband.

"Ready sweetheart?" Eric asked as he came into the room. He stopped when he saw Hadley in her dress. "You are breathtaking."

"Thanks daddy." Hadley said as she scooped up her bouquet and took Eric's arm.

They walked down the stairs and into the foyer. They had decided to have the wedding in the backyard as her parents and fellow Evolved had before them. When they made it out the back door a chill had begun to settle in the early evening air. It was unusual for a June evening to be this chilly. Hadley wondered momentarily if her nerves were messing with the temperature but shook it off when she saw Romulus standing at the head of the ceremony, ready to officiate her marriage to Thatcher.

She caught sight of Thatcher standing at the front of the ceremony and her heart skipped a beat. He smiled widely at her as he eagerly awaited her arrival. They began walking, every step bringing her closer to her future husband. All the nervousness she'd felt moments before disappeared as she closed the gap between them and her father gave her away to the love of her life.

Hadley didn't hear a word Romulus said. She was staring into Thatcher's gray eyes. He had to clear his throat when it was her turn to say her vows and exchange rings.

374

She felt her cheeks redden as the people in attendance chuckled at her. When they were announced as husband and wife they were both smiling like idiots. The reception and dance came and went all while Hadley was basking in the glow of her adoring husband.

The next morning, they headed to the airport to leave for their honeymoon. Despite the chill in the air, they were dressed for tropical weather. The temperatures would be much higher in Florida.

Chapter Forty-Seven: Kerr

The house felt empty after everyone had left. Tahlia and Eric had returned to Washington D.C. the same day Thatcher and Hadley left for their honeymoon. Dorian and Romulus had taken advantage of the empty house by heading out on a weeklong fishing trip. That left Kerr, Nora, Keira and Whitley with the large house all to themselves.

Nora and Whitley had decided they should play sardines. They had to explain the game to Kerr and Keira before they'd started. Kerr had never heard of this version of hide and seek; only one person hides while the others search for them, as each player finds the hidden person, they join them in their hiding spot until they are squished into a small space like sardines in a can. The first few rounds had been over quickly as they tried to make it easier for Keira. Of course, the little girl insisted that she was not a baby and did not need to be treated like a baby.

Unfortunately for Kerr, Nora had hidden first in the next round. Of course she had an unfair advantage with her abilities. The recent disappearance of Whitley indicated that the two were hiding together. Kerr wandered the hallways of the second level checking in each room. He heard a giggle coming from downstairs and assumed that Keira had found her mother and Whitley.

"If you're all together you might as well come out!" Kerr called as he made his way down the stairs.

No one answered him, so he continued in to the sitting room. He found Keira sitting in the window seat playing with some dolls.

"Hey sweet pea. Did you give up?" He asked.

"No, I'm just taking a break. My dolls were lonely." She said with a smile.

"Well, I'm going to keep looking for those two. We can't let them beat us just because mommy can hide in plain sight." Kerr whispered conspiratorially.

Keira giggled and put her dolls down to join her dad. Kerr took her small hand in his and pretended to sneak around doors and furniture. Keira laughed harder as he pulled her along behind him while over exaggerating his movements.

The pair made their way through the dining room and into the kitchen. They stopped briefly as Kerr grabbed a cookie for himself and Keira. He continued to sneak along the hallway toward the library, pausing every few steps to take an exaggerated bite from his cookie. Keira giggled at him the entire time. Kerr knew sneaking around was pointless as Nora and Whitley could be standing in the middle of the hallway for all he knew, but he was enjoying Keira's laughter.

As they made their way into the library, Kerr felt a difference in the air. It was thick with energy. He took another step into the room and looked around cautiously. This was not an energy he recognized; it wasn't negative, it was just different. He took another cautious step into the library and looked around.

"Nora? Whitley?" He called quietly.

Neither answered his call. He stuffed the last of his cookie in his mouth and took Keira's hand. She squeezed it tentatively to let him know that she felt his apprehension.

"Daddy, what is that?" Keira asked, pointing toward the bookshelf.

Kerr's eyes followed her arm to her pointing finger and saw a faint glow coming from a spot on the bookshelf.

"Nora! Whitley!" Kerr called out.

The tone of his voice must have told them the game was over because they appeared on either side of him. He glanced at Nora and Whitley and gestured towards the bookshelf.

"What the...." Whitley began but was cut off when the light intensified.

Books came flying from the shelf as the glow continued to increase. Kerr took another step forward as Whitley pulled Keira behind her. Nora must have decided it was time to call Dorian, but as she pulled out her phone, it began to ring.

"Hello?" Nora paused. "What?"

Kerr turned to look at his wife. Her tone had changed from interested to devastated in the span of two words. Nora was shaking her head and had a hand over her mouth.

"What is it?" Whitley asked placing a hand on Nora's shoulder.

Kerr turned his attention back to the bookshelf. He took the final few steps and reached for the source of the glow. He grabbed a book that was vibrating. When his hand emerged, he held the book of prophecies.

"When can you come home?" Nora asked the person on the phone. "Alright, I'll come get you soon."

Once she hung up she went to her favorite chair and sank down slowly. She appeared to be in a daze. Kerr was torn between the glowing book in his hand and the distraught look on his wife's face. They locked eyes for a moment.

"Avarice is awake." Nora said.

"The book is glowing." Kerr said.

"If this is a game of 'would you rather' do I get to weigh in?" Whitley asked.

Nora pulled her phone out again and called Dorian. "You need to pack up. I'm coming to get you. Something's happened."

Kerr looked back at the book in his hand. No one had mentioned the book of prophecies since Elpis had bound the Maladies. Kerr had no idea what was going on, but the Maladies had started waking up and that wasn't good.

"I need to go get everyone." Nora said numbly.

Nora disappeared leaving Kerr and Whitley standing in the library with a curious Keira.

"Daddy, why is that book glowing?" Keira asked.

Kerr shrugged and turned the book over in his hands. He examined the cover long enough to notice the glow was emanating from the symbols etched into the front that represented each of the Evolved. Suddenly, the book grew hot, hotter than his hands would allow him to touch. He dropped the book in surprise, hissing at the burning sensation it left on his hand.

"Kerr? What's going on?" Whitley asked stepping forward to get a better look.

"It burned me." Kerr replied simply, shaking his hand in the air.

"Daddy! The book is opening!" Keira shouted from her spot by the door.

Kerr turned his attention back to the book as the pages fluttered open. In a flurry of movement, the book stopped. Kerr leaned forward to read what was written on the page. He heard an intake of breath from Whitley as she read what was written on the page before them.

The New Era approaches.

Chapter Forty-Eight: Thatcher

They had seen Avarice while relaxing at Cocoa Beach. Hadley had leaned over to Thatcher and commented on the high maintenance chick with the blow-up mattress on the beach.

Thatcher laughed as they watched her meticulously set up her beach equipment. She blew up the air mattress with a battery operated pump, then laid her towel out on the mattress. She pulled a pop-up awning out of a carrying case and shook it once allowing it to open fully.

The woman wore a large sun hat with oversized black sunglasses. Her perfectly tanned skin was a strong contrast to her swimsuit with white and navy blue stripes. Her long blond hair was pulled into a perfect low ponytail at the base of her head; it looked like it had been freshly trimmed.

"That seems like a lot of work to enjoy a day at the beach." Hadley said quietly.

Thatcher nodded in amusement. The woman took off her hat and sunglasses and turned to head into the water. Hadley's sharp intake and strong grip on Thatcher's forearm told him she'd seen something she didn't like. He glanced at his wife and discovered she was staring openmouthed at the woman in the striped swimsuit. He swiveled his head back to look at the woman again and realized why Hadley was so terrified.

The hair, the perfect tan, the perfect white teeth as she smiled into the sun; this was Avarice.

"We need to go. Now. She doesn't know we've seen her." Hadley said with intensity.

Thatcher nodded and quickly helped pack up their lawn chairs and towels. They made their way to their hotel while Hadley called Nora.

Now, they sat waiting for Nora to arrive after having packed all their clothes and called the front desk for an early check out.

"I thought Dorian said we had plenty of time." Hadley said, breaking the silence between them.

"I thought so too." Thatcher said as he took Hadley into his arms.

They were standing in each other's arms when Nora cleared her throat.

"Sorry to interrupt. I figured I'd get you guys first. I haven't told Dorian and Romulus yet. I thought it best that you tell them." Nora told them. "Also, the book of prophecies is glowing."

Thatcher wrinkled his brow in concern. What did this all mean? Elpis had told the Old Immortals that they had many years before anything would happen. What had changed? He and Hadley had barely started their life together.

"You guys ready?" Nora asked.

They grabbed their bags and nodded. Nora put a hand on both of their arms and Thatcher felt the familiar tug in his belly button.

"Welcome back." Whitley said softly.

Thatcher and Hadley looked around to find Whitley, Keira and Kerr sitting on the couch, staring at them. He glanced to the coffee table and found the book of prophecies lying open.

"It opened a few minutes ago." Kerr told them.

Thatcher leaned forward and read the words scrawled across the page. His heart dropped when he realized what this meant. The sudden appearance of Avarice had set a series of events into motion that would bring about the New Era.

"What now?" Thatcher asked.

"Now, we gather the Virtues." Nora said.

Thatcher nodded as she disappeared. He and Hadley collapsed into a chair together and waited for the others to arrive.

Chapter Forty-Nine: Nora

"Dorian, we need to go." Nora said as soon as she arrived.

Dorian and Romulus were finishing packing up their fishing gear. Thankfully they had taken the tent down already and only needed to pack up their chairs and poles.

"What's happened Nora? Is everyone alright?" Romulus asked his voice thick with concern.

"Everyone is alright. But, you need to come back to the house. I've already brought Hadley and Thatcher back from their honeymoon." Nora said. "Is there anything you two would like to tell us regarding the book of prophecies?"

She was met with silence as the two exchanged a look of alarm.

"Why do you ask?" Dorian finally said.

"That's not an answer." Nora said as she helped them pick up the last of their gear.

Dorian sighed and closed his eyes for a moment in exasperation. "I know. We'll talk about it when we get home."

"Yeah well, Avarice is awake and the book is glowing, so you better be ready to fill in the blanks." Nora shot back.

That simple comment stopped the two Old Immortals in their tracks. They both stared at Nora for a moment before sharing a concerned look.

"We need to go now." Dorian said, placing a hand on her shoulder.

Romulus did the same and Nora transported them without another word. They arrived in the library in moments.

"I've got to get Tahlia and Eric." Nora told them.

Nora transported back with a guilty looking Tahlia and a confused but determined Eric. Nora strode over to stand with Kerr and the other Evolved.

"Alright, spill it." Nora said with her arms crossed.

"There are more prophecies." Dorian said.

Nora couldn't believe what she was hearing. How could the Old Immortals have kept this secret from them? She waited for them to explain more but there was nothing else.

"What are they about?" Hadley asked in the silence.

"We don't know." Tahlia told them.

"Elpis told us there would be more prophecies, but we were told we wouldn't know what they were until it was time." Romulus told them.

"Why?" Kerr asked.

"Because the Creator felt it would hold you all back from living your lives. We were supposed to have many years before this day came. I'd assumed you'd all have families of your own by the time we had to face the final battle." Dorian told them.

The book still lay open on the table. The simple sentence told them that they didn't have the years they'd anticipated. The New Era approaches. What did that mean? He didn't have to wait long for more information as more words scrawled across the page on their own.

The enemy will awaken and reunite; hope will evaporate leaving the world in a frozen state.

Death will sweep through the world, leaving devastation and doubt. The reactions of mankind will determine their fate.

Help will be found in the most surprising of places strengthening the Evolved for the final battle.

Only then will the Creator return to reclaim his creation.

Nora looked at the others as she finished reading the prophecies aloud for them to hear. Silence permeated the library as they shared concerned looks. Were the other

Maladies waking up in their hospital beds as they talked in the library?

"Well, we know the enemy has started to wake. That explains why the prophecies have now been revealed." Dorian said breaking the silence.

"But, the reason she put them all in different places was to keep them from seeing each other right?" Whitley asked.

"Yes, for now, they don't remember who they are. But if they see each other, it's all over. They'll band together to pull the rest from their amnesia." Kerr replied.

"For all we know, Avarice wouldn't have known who you were if she'd seen you. But we don't want to risk jogging her memory by seeing any of us." Dorian said.

Nora looked around the room. The last six months had been so easy. They'd gotten used to living a normal life, no impending battles or bad guys threatening them. Now as her eyes settled on her daughter she realized that her life would soon be in grave danger.

"We need to monitor them. We need to reactivate our scouts. It's time for a little recon. We can't just sit around wondering if or when the next Malady will awaken." Nora said firmly.

Murmurs of agreement came from around the room. Nora smiled at Keira as the little girl nodded her head at her mother. She knew Keira didn't entirely understand what was happening, but she knew enough to understand the seriousness of the situation. Nora's heart hurt as she looked at her little girl and thought about what the future held for her. The Maladies couldn't kill her, but the idea of them torturing her as they had Tahlia called to her most primal instincts to protect her young.

"Dorian, call the scouts. Get them briefed and ready." Nora instructed.

Dorian nodded and left the room.

"Romulus, Kerr, this is going to be much worse than what we've faced before. We need to know who will stand with the Creator and who will stand with the Maladies. I'll leave that to you." Nora said.

The two exchanged a look that indicated the weight of the work ahead but they nodded firmly at Nora.

"Tahlia, I need you and Eric on high alert. Any spikes in activities related to the Maladies must be reported back to us." Nora told Tahlia.

"Whitley, are you still able to communicate with the Council?" Nora asked.

"I haven't tried lately. Hold on." Whitley closed her eyes for just a moment, when they opened they were sparkling with excitement. She nodded her head.

"Good. We'll need their help." Nora said.

"Hadley, I need you to stay on top of any extreme changes in the weather. The constant chill in the air may very well be related to the coming battle." Nora instructed.

Her next instruction would be the hardest yet. She looked around at her family, smiling slightly when Dorian returned and gave her a thumbs up. She felt her chest tighten as she steeled herself for the onslaught of objections she was about to receive.

"Thatcher, I have a job for you too. I need you to take Keira somewhere safe." Nora said.

Shock and disbelief swept through the room as everyone uttered their objections. Thatcher kept his eyes locked on Nora's; the determination she saw reflected there told her he would do what needed to be done.

"What?" Kerr asked.

"No way!" Tahlia objected.

Nora held a hand up to stop them. "Keira cannot be captured. She cannot be subjected to the despicable acts the Maladies performed on Tahlia. I will not allow that to happen to my little girl."

Silence met her as her words sank in. Tahlia had tears running down her cheeks as Eric held her and rubbed her back. Kerr and Nora locked eyes and exchanged a silent agreement; their daughter would be safe no matter what. There were no further objections.

"She doesn't need to go yet. We won't need to be separated until at least two of the Maladies remember who they are. I don't think any of them would come after her on their own." Nora said.

"Where will I take her?" Thatcher asked.

"Eternity." Nora replied.

Epilogue

2017

"Keira! Are you ready? It's the first day of school! You don't want to be late." Kerr called up the stairs to his daughter.

Keira came bounding down the stairs in the purple jumper Tahlia handmade for her. Her dark curly hair had been pinned back to keep it from falling into her face. She smiled at her daddy and rushed to the kitchen for breakfast.

Kerr followed her and pulled out a box of her favorite cereal. He poured her a bowl and added milk, handing her a spoon as Nora came into view.

"Hi sweetheart! Are you excited for your first day as a first grader?" Nora asked as she kissed her daughter on top of the head.

"Yes! I can't wait to meet my new teacher." Keira said through a mouthful of cereal.

Both parents smiled warmly at their daughter and reminded her not to speak with her mouth full. Once she'd finished her breakfast, Nora and Kerr loaded her into the car and took off for the private school in Newall.

Dorian and Romulus waved them off from the driveway and went back inside to check in with their scouts. All the Maladies had awoken over the course of the last year and their scouts had been keeping close tabs on them every day. They received daily updates from Tahlia and Eric regarding potential signs of the Maladies returning to their old ways. So far, none of them knew who they really were.

Romulus and Kerr had spent a lot of time traveling the globe with Nora's help. The number of people they'd found that would stand by the Creator continued to grow, but so did the number of people who would support the Maladies. Their ability to read others had helped immensely, but so had the relationships they built with religious leaders from every denomination. It had been difficult at first as they told their story over and over to those leaders. Now that their history was known within religious circles, more and more supporters were coming forward. It hadn't been easy to share their history with others, but Kerr had learned how to share his visions of the past with true believers. Once he had shown a few people what they had done to protect the world it had created a domino effect.

The temperatures continued to stay much lower than they had been historically. Hadley had no power to control it, leading them to believe it was an indication of the first prophecy coming true. Both Romulus and Kerr had reported that the temperatures were significantly warmer in areas where they found concentrated numbers of the Creator's supporters. The temperature bordered on freezing in areas with higher crime rates and lower church attendance.

Thatcher had taken Nora's instructions to protect Keira very seriously and had even taken a custodial position at the school where Keira had attended kindergarten and would now be attending first grade. He was ready to get her out at a moment's notice.

When Nora and Kerr returned from dropping Keira off at school they found Dorian on the phone with one of their scouts. He had hung a large map on the wall behind his desk and was keeping track of the movements of each Malady. The troubled look on his face told them he had received some disconcerting news.

"And you're sure?" He asked. "Alright, keep tabs on them. I'll update everyone. Stay safe."

He hung up the phone and looked at the group that had gathered around him. Hadley, Nora, Kerr, Whitley and Romulus surrounded his desk. Dorian sighed deeply.

"Apparently Avarice and Rage signed up on one of those stupid dating websites. Their profiles matched and they're going on a lunch date in St. Louis today." He said with an irritated tone.

Kerr laughed despite the situation they were in. "What site was that? I hate everyone.com? Future world dominators.com?"

His laughter filled the room, and soon became infectious. Nora, Whitley and Hadley laughed themselves to tears. Even Romulus shook with laughter. Dorian stared around at them.

"Pull yourselves together. Do you know what this means?" Dorian asked sternly.

"Alright, alright, but seriously...what site did they meet on?" Kerr asked as he gulped in air.

"Hopeless romantics.com." Dorian said, knowing they'd recognize the irony.

Kerr bit his bottom lip and tried to hide the smile fighting its way to the surface. Nora cleared her throat.

"Well, that's actually a little sobering." Nora said.

They were silent for a moment. "Hopefully Avarice takes one look at Rage's ugly mug and decides to stand him up." Whitley said.

They all sat in the library waiting for the next call to come.

Thatcher and Keira arrived shortly after noon. Hadley filled Thatcher in on the call from the scout; he shared a strained look with Nora, understanding that he may need to take Keira away that day.

They were all eating macaroni and cheese when the phone rang. Dorian answered before the first ring finished.

"Hello?....Yes, and also with you." Dorian said, responding to the code word. "Has Avarice gone in yet?....Okay, stay on the line with me until she does."

The others waited, hanging on every word as Dorian put the phone on speaker.

"Rage is sitting at a table waiting. Avarice is coming down the sidewalk." The scout said. "She's going in."

They waited, none of them daring to breathe or speak.

"They're shaking hands." He whispered, the intensity in his voice rising as he watched.

"They've recognized each other. Avarice is clearly disgusted. Rage just threw the table. The people inside are terrified, but they're leaving the restaurant. I better get out of here."

"Thank you Steve, be safe." Dorian said as he hung up.

They all looked at each other for a few moments, saying a million things in their silence. Nora and Kerr held Keira close, Thatcher stood protectively next to them while holding Hadley's hand. Whitley was hugging herself, eyes closed, listening to the Council of Immortals. Dorian and Romulus locked eyes, they were getting older but they weren't done fighting.

"It's begun." Whitley said, breaking the silence.

GROWING hope

Watch for the final book in

The New Era Saga coming 2016.

CHOOSING eternity

About the Author:

KT Webb is a big city girl living in small town South Dakota with her husband and two children. She believes in the power of words and enjoys writing stories that make the impossible seem possible. By day, KT is a marketing and communications professional; by night, she is a passionate independent author.

KT loves reading, listening to pop-punk music (especially when she's writing), having adventures with her children and traveling. She believes in magic, that there's a hero inside everyone and that characters should be just as flawed and intriguing as the people we meet every day.

A Note from the Author:

Thank you for reading Growing Hope! I truly hope you are enjoying The New Era Saga so far. I cannot wait to share the final installment with you all. Look for it to come out next year. Tell others what you think by leaving a review on Amazon.com and/or Goodreads.com

I love to hear from my fans;

Website: www.ktwebbauthor.com

Email: kt_webb@hotmail.com

Follow me on Twitter: @_KT_Webb_

Like my Facebook page: KT Webb.